Bollywood
CONFIDENTIAL

By Sonia Singh

BOLLYWOOD CONFIDENTIAL
GODDESS FOR HIRE

Sonia SINGH

Bollywood CONFIDENTIAL

AVON
TRADE

An Imprint of HarperCollins*Publishers*

HarperCollins books may be purchased for educational, business, or sales promotional use. For information please write: Special Markets Department, HarperCollins Publishers Inc., 10 East 53rd Street, New York, NY 10022.

FIRST EDITION

Interior text designed by Diahann Sturge

Library of Congress Cataloging-in-Publication Data

Singh, Sonia.
   Bollywood confidential / by Sonia Singh.—1st ed.
      p. cm.
ISBN 0-06-059038-6 (acid-free paper)
1. East Indian American women—Fiction.   2. Motion picture actors and actresses—Fiction.   3. Motion picture industry—Fiction.   4. Americans—India—Fiction.   5. Bombay (India)—Fiction.   I. Title.

PS3619.I5745B65 2005
813'.6—dc22   2004029182

05 06 07 08 09 JTC/RRD 10 9 8 7 6 5 4 3 2 1

This book is dedicated to my father, Bhupindar Aujla Singh, affectionately known as Bob. If it wasn't for you, Dad, I never would have made it to Bombay. Thank you for making the whole Bollywood experience happen.

Mom, thank you for instilling in me a love for all things Bollywood. Masala moviemaking has no bigger fan than you.

Acknowledgments

Kimberly Whalen: my fabulous agent, who could give any hip-thrusting Bollywood heroine a run for her money.

Lyssa Keusch: my wonderful editor, who surely must have been Indian in her past life, because the woman has curry running through her veins

Many thanks to the stellar team at Avon Trade: Carrie Feron, May Chen, Pamela Spengler-Jaffee, Rachel Fershleiser and Jamie Beckman. You guys rock!

And to the original Stressed-out Sadhu:

Ram Uncle, you've provided me with more inspiration than you can ever imagine. Bombay would never have been the same without you.

Prologue

Raveena Rai once believed there was nothing worse than being a D-list actress in Hollywood.

But that was before she found herself crouched on the dirt floor of a Bombay slum, inhaling fecal matter fumes and frightened beyond belief because she was on the run from the Indian police.

Back in LA, the most frightening thing in her life had been discovering she'd mistakenly eaten carbohydrates while on the Atkins diet.

Now she faced incarceration in an Indian prison.

Personally, Raveena would rather leap off Mt. Everest—provided she could make it across India's border and into Nepal.

She longed to be back in her Santa Monica condo, drinking a vodka tonic and writing practice acceptance speeches for her Oscar for Best Actress or Best Supporting Actress.

Whichever came first.

Regarding the vodka tonic, Raveena worried about eating carbs . . . not *drinking* them.

She moved from crouching to a curled-up fetal position. The heavy night air caused trickles of sweat and grime to run down her face.

But this was no time to think about the havoc wreaked on her pores.

A near hysterical giggle slipped from her lips as she visualized the expression on her dermatologist's face. "But Raveena, how could you be on the run without sunblock, an oil-free moisturizer and a good eye cream?"

But before she could lapse into a bout of panic-stricken chuckles, the sound of voices erupted from outside.

Loud male voices.

The police had found her.

Desperately, she looked around for a place to hide.

Rather difficult in a shanty one-sixteenth the size of a studio apartment in New York City. The only furniture in the room was a shabby straw mat.

This was no time to be choosy, so she scuttled across the floor and began wriggling her way under the covering just as the door burst open.

Uniformed men with flashlights filled the room and yanked off her hiding place.

She placed a weak hand in front of her eyes to shield them from the glare of the lights.

This was the end.

All twenty-eight years of her life flashed before her.

Well, okay, maybe just the last six months.

Every single event that had led up to her coming to Bombay.

And a place known simply as . . .

Bollywood.

Chapter 1

Six months earlier . . .

Raveena was seriously getting tired of her agent.

He ushered her into his Wilshire Boulevard office and into a black art deco chair shaped like a swan, which was definitely designed without the input of any self-respecting chiropractor. Sure enough, the moment she sat down she felt her back begin to spasm.

Griffin smiled. "I'm so sorry I haven't returned your calls. In between snorkeling in the Caribbean and yachting in the Mediterranean, I haven't had a moment to sit down."

Raveena had spent the holidays pouring half a bottle of brandy into her eggnog.

She felt a wave of depression wash over her.

Raveena wasn't normally a depressed person. She always tried to see the bright side of things. Sometimes it took a day or even a decade to see the silver lining, but at least she kept on trying.

Therapy helped.

Denial helped more.

Because it seemed the "LA" thing to do, Raveena had made an appointment with a well-known psychiatrist in Malibu. Unfortunately, the good doctor hadn't appreciated it when halfway through their session Raveena tentatively raised her hand and said, "Instead of talking, could we get to the prescribing?"

Basically, as if the month of January weren't gloomy enough, her acting career—to put it politely—was in the proverbial shit hole.

Griffin smiled again, and this time the effect nearly blinded her. Raveena knew she had good teeth—everyone in the Rai family did—but next to Griffin her pearly whites looked positively saffron.

Across from her, Griffin leaned back in his black leather chair, ran his fingers through his perfectly tousled red hair, and proceeded to wax eloquent about the fabulous role she simply *had* to try out for. "It's a career-making role, Raveena," he said.

It was always a career-making role.

As if she expected him to present her with a career-obliterating offer.

Griffin Bish had been Raveena's agent for seven years, ever since she'd moved to Los Angeles at the tender age of twenty-one. Some people may not have considered the move a big deal since she'd grown up just forty-five minutes away in Newport Beach. After all, it wasn't like she was some fresh-faced farm girl from Iowa hopping the bus in Des Moines, coming to LA with her dreams in her jeans pocket.

Or was it?

Orange County and Los Angeles may be neighbors, but they're worlds apart. On the surface, the two locations seem similar, like a glass of water and a glass of vodka, but then you take a sip . . .

Speaking of vodka, she thought longingly of the Stoli stashed in her freezer.

"Raveena, the role is to die for," Griffin insisted.

Her left butt cheek had grown numb and she shifted.

"You'll play one of two slave girls assigned to the emperor," he added. They want someone ethnic-looking. It's not a speaking part—"

She sighed. "Naturally."

"But you'll be able to do a lot of emoting with your eyes."

Right.

Seven years in Hollywood and she'd played a gypsy girl, a belly dancer, a Mexican cocktail waitress . . .

And those were the roles worth mentioning.

To be fair, it wasn't really Griffin's fault. Despite the success of films like *Monsoon Wedding* and *Bend It Like Beckham* in the west, Hollywood wasn't exactly teeming with roles for women of Indian origin.

Make that East Indian origin.

Thanks to geographically challenged Columbus, Raveena had once been sent on a casting call where the producers were looking for an Indian woman. Upon arriving, she'd discovered that by Indian they meant Pocahontas, not Parvati.

Anyway, in Raveena's expert opinion, her golden coloring should afford her a variety of roles. After all, she'd been mistaken for women of Hispanic, Arabic and Southern Italian origin. The problem was the number of available Hispanic,

Arabic, Southern Italian and East Indian roles combined could fit in the tear duct of her right eye.

Besides, there were enough Hispanic and Italian actresses out there to fill their respective parts. Raveena knew the likelihood of a casting agent selecting her, when Salma Hayek and Jennifer Lopez were ready and willing, was about as likely as a foreign-born action star becoming governor of California.

Oh wait . . .

Taking a deep breath, Raveena forcibly gulped down her pride. "When's the audition?"

Griffin flashed another blinding smile.

This was Hollywood, remember?

Chapter 2

One week later Raveena had tried out for the role of slave girl, lost it to a Brazilian bikini model, nearly twisted her ankle in a pilates class and stubbed her toe in yoga.

About the Brazilian model, apparently the casting director was looking for a more marketable minority.

Try saying that three times fast.

To top it all off, it was Saturday night and she was having dinner with her parents.

Truth be told, she didn't mind hanging out with them. It's just that a long, long time ago in a place far, far away, she recalled spending her Saturday nights with dates.

Sometimes when she was in extreme periods of denial— yes, her favorite word—she convinced herself that she'd sacrificed her love life for her career.

It was called ambition.

It was also called eight years later and no career or boyfriend to speak of.

Almost on cue, Mr. and Mrs. Rai walked up to the restaurant.

Raveena's father, as usual, was dressed in a three-piece suit, silk handkerchief visible in a neat triangle in his breast pocket. If he could, he would wear a three-piece suit every day of his life.

He also liked wearing women's perfume, but this was neither the time nor the place to go into that.

This time the suit was charcoal gray, the tie and handkerchief were burgundy, and the scent was Opium, if she wasn't mistaken.

Her mother was dressed in an elegant gold sari. Her shoulder-length hair was loose, and a stunning gold and pearl choker graced her slender neck. Matching chandelier earrings dangled from her small ears. She was a beauty.

People had often told Raveena that she looked like her mother, and she supposed it was true, but with some very discernible differences. Her mother was barely an inch over five feet and slender as a willow.

At five-six, Raveena was sturdy as an oak. Raveena's shoe size was also five sizes bigger than her mother's, which made walking around in stiletto heels a form of torture not condemned by the United Nations.

Meanwhile, her mother's tiny feet would have made a nineteenth-century Chinese noblewoman drool with envy.

Yes, her parents were different.

And not just because they were committed curry consumers.

First of all, Raveena's father came from a very devout Sikh family, yet his parents chose to name him Bob. Raveena's mother was Hindu and named Leela after a famous Indian actress who happened to kill herself by downing a bottle of Johnny Walker and jumping off the tallest building in Bombay.

Then again, Raveena's elder brother Rahul always said they were just your typical Indian immigrant family.

Speaking of Rahul, Raveena suddenly wished he were joining them tonight. Rahul was in international banking and had been promoted from the Manhattan office to Brussels. She'd stayed with him last summer and met his girlfriend, Brigitta, who cooed endearments to Rahul in Flemish.

Rahul was four years older than Raveena, and she honestly believed her parents would have refused to let her major in theater arts if it weren't for him. Because by the time she was ready for college, Bob and Leela were under the blissful delusion that their one and only daughter would be studying accounting.

Please don't ask her where they got that idea!

When they realized Raveena wanted to forgo accounting for acting, they didn't just hit the roof, they demolished it.

Rahul—about to graduate summa cum laude from Stanford—flew to Orange County and sat the Rai family down for a talk. He explained to their parents that acting was his sister's dream and she would be unhappy doing anything else.

They were unmoved and unimpressed. Bob stared pointedly at his watch.

Rahul then pointed out that as an investment banker he would see to Raveena's financial security if the need should arise.

Their parents visibly thawed.

Rahul then winked at Raveena and added that he would

be sure to introduce his equally successful fellow banker friends to his little sister.

The tension in the room broke and slowly disappeared. Although for some reason their father continued to stare at his watch.

In that moment, Raveena felt like she'd won the sibling lottery.

Bob was hungry, so they entered the restaurant and followed the statuesque blond to their table. Raveena couldn't resist a small thrill of satisfaction. They were at Mantra—a hip new LA restaurant that specialized in Indian-Californian fusion cuisine. Because her last name wasn't Coppola, she'd had to book the table three weeks in advance.

Still brimming with bubbles of satisfaction, Raveena smiled at the blond.

The blond did not return it.

This was Santa Monica. The waiters and waitresses all had headshots. And customer service was not listed on their resumes.

Determined to enjoy the night, Raveena sat down and kept the smile on her face with all the determination of a beauty pageant contestant. Tonight was her mother's birthday. They were celebrating.

Though based on past experiences out to dinner with her family, she reflected that the only people who'd really be celebrating were the ones at the other tables.

Leela gracefully adjusted the folds of her sari and gazed around. Suddenly her nose began wrinkling furiously like a rabid bunny. "What is that smell?"

Raveena took a sniff. "Curry powder I think."

Her mother raised an elegant eyebrow. "You think I don't know what curry powder smells like?"

Okay, Raveena was seriously doubting her choice of restaurant. What on Earth had made her think her parents would like Mantra?

The fact that there were more Indian artifacts lining the restaurant walls than in the entire state of Punjab? Or perhaps it was how the number of gauzy glittery scarves draped around the tables could easily outfit several dozen harems?

And did they really need to be situated so close to the sitar player?

Speaking of the musician, he had a mane of curly brown hair and began strumming the sitar version of a Jessica Simpson song. Bob indiscreetly covered his ears.

The waiter appeared and Raveena decided it was time to take advantage of Mantra's fully stocked bar.

"Double vodka martini," she said.

Her mother stared until Raveena felt tiny pinpricks of maternal disapproval penetrate the top layer of her skin. "You drink too much," Leela scolded.

"No I don't."

That was pretty much the end of their discussion.

For the next few moments, her father quietly sipped his merlot, her mother quietly fumed, and Raveena quietly decided the evening was going far better than planned.

The silence was short-lived as Leela set down the menu and frowned. "Why did we have to come all the way to LA? I could have cooked dinner for us."

"Because it's your birthday, Mom," Raveena said. The idea is for you to get out and have some fun. This place is happening. We'll probably see some celebrities."

Leela's interest perked. "Like Paul Newman?"

"Ah, I don't really think it's his scene, but Leonardo DiCaprio has been spotted regularly."

She snorted. "That little boy from *Titanic*? He looks like a woman."

Leela didn't have a hankering for actors, unless they were of the Bollywood variety. Bollywood—for those not in the know—is the popular term used to describe the Indian film industry. Bombay plus Hollywood equals Bollywood.

Then again, she supposed the word was debatable considering the name of the city had officially been changed from Bombay to Mumbai in 1997.

Mumbollywood didn't exactly roll off the tongue.

Not that it mattered. Most of the world continued to refer to the city as Bombay.

The waiter was hovering near the table, so Raveena cracked open the menu with determination. "I'm having the prawn curry. Mom?"

Frowning, Leela peered at the menu. "These dishes are weird. Tandoori pizza? Tofu curry? This isn't Indian food." As if to illustrate her point, she began examining the plates of poppadum and bowls of chutney on the table with suspicion.

Trying to ignore her mother's scowling face, Raveena turned to her father. "What do you feel like, Dad? The lamb here is really good."

Bob smoothed the ends of his mustache and cleared his throat. "Are we talking New Zealand lamb? That's the best. If the lamb here came from China, I'm not touching it. I'd rather eat shit."

Raveena was spared from asking her father if he'd like a

salad with that when her cell phone began to ring. She dug it out of her purse. "Hello?"

"Raveena, doll, it's Griffin."

"Who's calling?" Leela demanded.

"My agent," Raveena whispered.

"I want to talk to him. Why isn't he setting you up with Spielberg and that nice Indian boy who made the movie about ghosts?"

She meant M. Night Shyamalan, director of *The Sixth Sense*.

Call her crazy, but Raveena didn't think putting her mother on the phone with her agent was a good idea.

Griffin persisted. "Raveena? Hello? Are you listening?"

She looked over at her parents who, instead of looking at each other, were watching the diners at the next table.

Maybe it was a good time for her mother to begin opening presents.

"Look, Griffin," she said quickly. "I'll call you back. I'm in the middle of—"

His voice rose in volume. "We can't talk later. We're talking leading role here! We're talking major film! You're up for it! In fact, you're perfect for it!"

Her mouth dropped open.

"Close your mouth, Raveena," her mother scolded. "Otherwise, you look slow."

Raveena turned away and pressed the cell phone close to her ear. Excitement began to thud inside her. "A leading role?" It couldn't be. After all these years . . . "Who's the director? The producer?"

"Randy Kapoor is producing and directing," Griffin said.

She was puzzled. "Randy? I've never heard of him."

Raveena thought she knew all the Hollywood players of Indian descent. She belonged to a group called the South Asian Representation Society or SARS.

Sidenote: They existed before the global disease.

She jogged her memory. "Oh wait. Is this the guy with Buddha Tree Productions? The one making the Tibetan film with Richard Gere?"

Visions of co-starring with the gorgeous Gere swirled through her head, and she nearly floated out of her chair with giddiness.

Griffin cleared his throat. "Perhaps I didn't make myself clear. This isn't a Hollywood film."

"Sorry?"

"It's Bollywood."

She promptly fell back to Earth. "Bollywood?" she shrieked.

"Bollywood?" Her father echoed.

Leela's eyes lit up and she smiled for the first time all night. "Bollywood?"

Maybe Raveena had just given her mother the birthday present of a lifetime.

Chapter 3

After dinner Raveena returned in a daze to her small Santa Monica condo.

She parked her Toyota Prius—the hybrid of choice for all Hollywood types—and let herself in.

Pouring a vodka and Red Bull, she retreated to the living room—a mere three steps—and curled up in her favorite purple velvet chair.

Staring at the praline-colored walls, decorated with framed posters of her favorite movies like *Roman Holiday*, *The Godfather* and *Raiders of the Lost Ark*, she thought about the Bollywood offer.

Bollywood.

Even as a kid she hadn't been able to stand watching Indian movies.

The bloodstains on the heroes' clothes always looked like ketchup. The heroines wore too much makeup. And just when you thought you'd finally figured out how the hero could possibly leap across an entire row of supply trucks in his white loafers with three-inch heels, the entire cast would abruptly break into a song-and-dance sequence.

Leela—an avowed Bollywood fanatic—didn't appreciate her daughter's continuous critical commentary and pointed out that some of Raveena's favorite movies were musicals like *Grease, The Sound of Music* and *Moulin Rouge.*

Raveena's response was to thrust out her pelvis and begin shaking her hips in imitation of the Bollywood babes on screen.

Before tonight, Raveena would have thought Bollywood had as much relevance to her world as the Kabbalah did to a devout Muslim.

Downing her drink, she rinsed the glass and placed it in the dishwasher. Then it was time to begin her nightly ministrations.

Securing her hair with a headband, she sat down in front of her bedroom dresser and began removing her makeup. She followed that up with a sugar-based exfoliating scrub.

A tedious ritual and one she'd only just begun.

Sometimes Raveena wanted to say to hell with it and jump into bed, face dirty, teeth un-flossed, but then a vision of Angelina Jolie or Kate Winslet would surface in her head, and she'd remember the stars she was up against.

So, as she battled dead skin cells and misbehaving pores, she went over the remaining details Griffin had filled her in on after her mother's excited outburst at the restaurant.

There was one aspect that had startled her most:

No audition.

She couldn't believe there was no audition for the role.

Only people like Meryl Streep and Robert De Niro (known as Bob in the biz) had roles hand delivered to them.

Not Raveena Rai.

But apparently the director, Randy Kapoor, while in Singapore attending an international Bollywood awards show, had seen a commercial she'd starred in.

The commercial was for a super-absorbent Japanese tampon the length and width of a toothpick.

The Vagitsu.

Don't visualize it.

Two years before, India had won the Miss Globe crown—similar to the Miss Universe title—for the first time. Indian fever struck Japan, and the Vagitsu Company had approached Miss Globe to star in its ad campaign.

She declined.

Apparently, Miss Globe did not want to embarrass her traditional Indian family by appearing in a tampon commercial.

Raveena had no such qualms.

After an international casting call, she was flown first class to Tokyo, put up in a five-star hotel and spent a week on a set that was straight out of Mira Nair's *Kama Sutra*. For seven days she wore a number of gauzy outfits, shot sultry looks into the camera, and was paid more money than she'd ever seen in her life.

For her efforts, she also received a lifetime supply of the Vagitsu.

Truly a fabulous product and now the number one tampon in all of Asia.

FDA approval is still pending in the United States.

Anyway, thanks to that commercial, which was still

running, Raveena was able to afford a trendy one-bedroom condo in Santa Monica instead of a cockroach-infested studio in North Hollywood, *and* get presented with a Bollywood acting offer on a silver platter.

All without auditioning.

Speaking of the role, she only had a brief sketch of the story. It revolved around an American girl of Indian heritage who grows up without a father. It's only when her mother is on her deathbed that the heroine discovers her father is very much alive and living in a small village in India.

Before the heroine can react, the mother offers up another deathbed confession. The father has no idea that his daughter even exists. The mother then conveniently—for the storyline—dies. The heroine, who has never been to India, ends up hopping a plane determined to find her father.

No mention of whether she gets her malaria shots or not.

Of course, after three days in India she realizes there's more than one village in the country. So she hires a tour guide, the hero. The hero and heroine begin their journey across India looking for dear lost Daddy, slowly falling in love and facing many adventures and sticky situations along the way. One of which involves a nasty-tempered camel and multiple molestations by a monkey.

When the heroine finally reunites with her father, there is much singing and much crying, as the old man is also on his deathbed. However, finding out that he has a daughter gives him the will to live.

Raveena could play the role in her sleep.

Beauty routine finally over, she threw on her favorite

pink cotton nightshirt, slipped in between the sheets and closed her eyes.

Call her crazy, but she couldn't decide what to do.

Bollywood was so . . . far.

It was time to talk this over with her friends.

Chapter 4

Siddharth was the number one actor in India.

But he couldn't care less.

He was bored.

High above the trees of Bombay, ensconced in the pent-house flat he shared with his mother and sister, having just returned from a week-long shoot in Mauritius, Siddharth leaned back in the recliner, stretched out his long legs and began flipping through channels on the new flat-screen TV.

One of his movies was airing on the Zee Network. He grimaced, and it wasn't from the chicken tikka masala that Pratab—the family cook—had prepared for dinner.

On screen, Siddharth got down on one knee and began shaking his shoulders to the beat of the music.

His grimace deepened into a scowl.

He was thirty-two, for God's sake. How much longer would he have to play the boyish college heartthrob?

Siddharth flipped channels and came upon another of his films. This time he was running through a field of tulips in Holland, his arms outstretched, beaming from ear to ear, flashing his famous toothy smile.

Siddharth remembered a time when acting had been his passion. Now all he did was star in film after film about lovers who came together, were torn apart, and then brought together again at the end.

He'd finally taken a risk last year and starred in a film where he'd played the villain.

He'd had the time of his life.

But the film had bombed at the box office.

Siddharth's status as an A-list actor remained untouched, but he'd learned that the Indian audience wanted to see him as a romantic hero and would settle for nothing else.

Ever since Siddharth's father had passed away when he was sixteen and his sister Sachi just a baby, he'd become the sole financial support for his mother and sister. He couldn't afford to take chances with his career.

Disgusted with watching himself, he turned off the TV and closed his eyes.

Chapter 5

"Unlike you, Jai, not everyone was sexually active in the womb."

Raveena said this last comment a bit too loudly, and the man on the street corner gave her a startled look.

She returned the look, because he had an iguana perched on each one of his shoulders and one on top of his head.

Los Angeles. Love it or hate it.

It was Sunday afternoon, they were driving into West LA, and she had just finished telling her two best friends, Jai and Maza, about the Bollywood role.

Somehow the conversation had segued into Jai's sex life.

Then again, a conversation about blueberry muffins could take a sexual turn if Jai was around.

Maza and Jai finished their cigarettes and put the stubs into the biodegradable baggie Maza always carried in her car.

Raveena wasn't a smoker and had opened the window. Now that the air was clear she closed it. She didn't want to freak out any more people with their conversation.

Jai and Raveena had been friends forever. Their parents

moved in the same Indian social circle. The year the two friends had turned twenty-one, Jai had come out to her.

Personally, Raveena had been more surprised by the zit she discovered on her chin that very same morning.

As much as she loved him, Jai was under the serious delusion that most people thought he was straight.

He was also paranoid that his parents would one day discover his secret sexual identity.

Raveena didn't have the heart to tell Jai that it was pretty obvious from the way his parents never brought up their son's lack of girlfriends, his career as a makeup artist at MAC, or his DVD collector's edition of the show *Queer as Folk*, that they probably had a clue.

In the backseat, Jai pointed at the well-muscled blond man in a red convertible. "You think he's into chicken tandoori?"

Maza pressed a hand to her stomach. "Stop. You're making me hungry."

Jai caught Raveena's eye and winked. "I wasn't talking about food, honey."

She didn't wink back. "Can we please get back to discussing the Bollywood deal?"

They were now stuck in a traffic jam on Sunset Boulevard. Only in Southern California could you find yourself in a traffic jam on a Sunday afternoon.

"Personally, I'd love to get out of LA," Maza said. "Go to a spiritual place like India and just live in a cave."

Ah . . . not!

Maza gunned the engine of her Range Rover and pushed forward in traffic.

Maza, the first friend Raveena had made after moving to

LA, donated numerous hours to cleaning up the environment yet drove one of the most expensive SUVs on the market.

Go figure.

At least she was an excellent driver, which was more than Raveena could say for most SUV owners.

One summer, just for the hell of it, Maza had driven a fourteen-wheeler across country. She claimed there was something Zen-like about truck driving.

Raveena would imagine Maza, dressed head to toe in Donna Karan, cigarette dangling from her lips, Chanel sunglasses protecting her eyes, CB radio squawking, as she drove the behemoth of a vehicle all the way from California to New Hampshire.

Maza was beautiful and seemed annoyed by the fact. She had an ivory complexion, thick black hair and catlike dark eyes. Regardless of the season, she always swathed herself from head to toe in black. For instance, on this gorgeous January day, Maza had on a black turtleneck and a black sweater.

It was seventy degrees and sunny.

Go figure.

Maza was a writer and her first novel had been released last year. The book detailed the dark nihilistic journey of a woman tortured by life and her deepening mental disease. The story had left Raveena vaguely disturbed. The gothic fans that routinely showed up at Maza's book signings left her even more disturbed and slightly frightened.

A few months ago, one of Maza's male fans had begun stalking her. He had confronted her in the middle of the night outside her cottage nestled deep inside the Hollywood Hills.

When he'd grabbed her and demanded her undying love, Maza had calmly kicked her attacker in the crotch and dialed 911 on her cell phone, all without dropping her cigarette. She'd coolly continued to smoke, her boot firmly planted on the man's neck as he lay prone and groaning, until the police arrived.

Maza and Raveena met in a bookstore. Maza had been browsing in Witchcraft and Demonology when Raveena accidentally knocked over a stack of books titled *Women Who Don't Hate Enough*. Maza had come over to help her restock them, and they'd been friends ever since.

Maza forgave Raveena's occasional buying of a Britney Spears album.

Raveena forgave Maza cleansing her aura with sage before she stepped into her house.

Go figure.

Despite all of their oddities, Raveena was grateful the three of them were so close. For instance, here they were taking her to the Standard Lounge on Sunset to celebrate the Bollywood role.

The one she hadn't yet agreed to.

"Can we get back to my dilemma?" Raveena asked. "I can't just pack up and leave LA. They want me to commit to six months in Bombay. What if a great opportunity comes my way in Hollywood?"

Jai leaned forward. "Pardon me, sweetie, but what LA career? You've been waiting for a 'great opportunity' for seven years!"

She sighed and leaned her head back against the seat. Jai had a point. Maza, umm, sort of did too. What was holding her back? A personal dislike of Bollywood films? Her dream of becoming the next Gwyneth Paltrow?

Maza shot Raveena a sidelong glance. "You're thinking about Gwyneth Paltrow, aren't you?"

"How'd you know?"

"You're always thinking about Gwyneth," Jai said. "You constantly compare yourself to her."

"Well, we're the same age, and she's an Oscar-winning actress."

Jai yawned. "No one of Indian descent is going to win an Oscar. We just don't get those types of roles."

Raveena disagreed. "What about Ben Kingsley? He's Indian and he won an Oscar."

"He's half," Jai said.

"So? I'll change my name to Raveena Queensley and say I'm half too." Mentally, she apologized to her parents for disowning their heritage.

Maza thumped her horn and switched lanes. "Anthony Quinn," she said suddenly, checking her rearview mirror.

Jai's head whipped around. "Where? Where?"

"He passed away in 2001, Jai," Raveena clarified.

Maza gave the driver behind her the finger, and then proceeded to explain. "Anthony Quinn was half Mexican and half Irish. He struggled for years in Hollywood, but no one would cast him as a leading man. Finally he got an offer from an Italian director. So, does he go off to Italy and start making movies there, or does he stick it out in Hollywood?"

"Italian men are so hot," Jai said dreamily.

"Anyway," Maza continued, "Anthony moved to Italy

and began working in the industry. People back home told him he was ruining his career. They told him there was no way starring in Italian films was going to help him in Hollywood. But Anthony eventually became the number one actor in Italy with fans all across the country. They were mad about him."

"How do you know so much about Anthony Quinn?" Jai questioned.

"I had writer's block and ended up watching his biography on A&E."

Jai sighed. "He was a gorgeous man, wasn't he?"

"But back to my story," Maza said, quickly cutting across the lane, swerving right and somehow bypassing ninety percent of the traffic. "Because of Quinn's status as an Italian idol, Hollywood finally took notice." She pulled up in front of the Standard and put the car in park. "And the rest, chica, is history."

They all filed out, and the valet guy jumped into the car. Anthony Quinn's story left Raveena quiet. She'd assumed the man had arrived in Hollywood and become an overnight sensation.

Well, Raveena really wasn't that naïve, but she hadn't realized the famous actor had to make a side trip to Italy on his journey to Hollywood.

Jai put his arm around Raveena. "So, what do you think? I hear Bollywood fans number almost a billion."

Maza pulled a pack of Marlboros out of her bag. "Really?"

Jai gallantly held open the door and ushered them into the famous shag-carpeted, bubble chair-decorated lobby.

Raveena recalled an article her mother had once read her. "I think he's right. India's population is now practically a billion. Add to that the millions of Indian immigrants scattered throughout the UK, Canada, the United States, Australia, Asia and Africa." Her mother's words swirled through her head. "And Bollywood fans aren't just Indians. Russians, Armenians, Israelis, Turks, Arabs, Japanese, Chinese, Malaysians, Thai . . . they all watch Bollywood films."

Maza stopped in the lobby and turned to face her. "Now, before we hit the bar, what'll we be toasting to?"

Raveena couldn't help smiling. "I'll do it."

Looked like she was going Bollywood!

Jai threw his arms around her and planted a big kiss on her cheek. Raveena was pretty sure it was the first time he'd kissed a member of the opposite sex in five years.

Maza nodded and lit up a cigarette. The concierge spied her, frowned and came running over.

Raveena was moving to Bombay.

Chapter 6

"*India is a dirty stinking place. Too many stinking people. Bad smells. Why go there?*"

Waiting for Raveena's reaction to her comment, Auntie Kiran stuffed a samosa from the plate on the table into her mouth and began chewing furiously.

Raveena had dropped by her parents' house to pick up some Bollywood DVDs. She figured she may as well watch some of the latest releases.

Merely for research purposes, of course.

Unfortunately she'd chosen the very afternoon her mother was holding her weekly kitty party. Basically, a group of Indian aunties got together at a restaurant or at one another's homes. Their game was Gin Rummy. Everyone anteed up, and the entire kitty went to the winner.

The dining table was practically buckling with the weight of all the snacks it was supporting: nachos, samosas, chicken tandoori tenders, cheesecake, chips and several varieties of dips and chutneys. And in the center of it all was Auntie Kiran—a very competitive card player.

Kiran wasn't technically Raveena's aunt, but her mother's best friend. She was short with chubby cheeks and frizzy hair dyed an unnatural burgundy shade. Whether at the travel agency she owned or at a party, Aunt Kiran habitually wore brightly colored sweatpants and decorated her ears, nose, throat and wrists with heavy gold jewelry.

Leela laughed. "Come on, Kiran, it's not that bad."

Taking a seat, Raveena helped herself to a piece of chicken and dipped it into the nacho cheese. "What about the Taj Mahal? People from all over the world go to India just to see that."

Auntie Kiran scoffed and Raveena had to dodge a chunk of potato that came flying out of her mouth. "Taj Mahal? Big deal! Go to Atlantic City. See the Trump Taj Mahal. Much better. And it has clean bathrooms."

Auntie Bindo, who read palms as a hobby and enjoyed playing practical jokes on her children (she once hid in the laundry room and jumped out of the hamper, scaring them to death), nudged Raveena. "Did you get your shots?"

Before she could answer, Auntie Kiran butted in, "What's the point of getting shots? Indian germs are too strong. They'll latch onto her clean American blood."

"Make sure you drink only bottled water," Raveena's mother told her for the hundredth time.

Auntie Kiran scoffed. "Bottled water isn't safe. Tourists have been getting all manner of diseases from bottled water that was really taken from the sewer."

Sewers?

Raveena had an aversion to drinking out of public water fountains because of the germs.

At that moment, Auntie Bindo slammed down her cards and shouted "Gin Rummy!"

Auntie Kiran whipped around, pointed a stubby finger, and accused her of cheating.

The table erupted into shouts and recriminations, and suddenly chutney became a projectile weapon.

Ducking her head, Raveena raced from the room and took refuge on the front steps outside.

Sitting down, she could still hear shouting from inside and scooted farther away from the door. Putting thoughts of Auntie Kiran and bottled sewage out of her head, she dialed Griffin's office.

As it turned out, Griffin was wearing a blue cashmere sweater that brought out the blue in his eyes.

No, Raveena wasn't psychic. The first thing Griffin said to her after hello was, "Raveena, doll, the blue cashmere sweater I'm wearing absolutely brings out the blue of my eyes."

"I'm sure it does, Griffin," she answered. Meanwhile, according to her mother, the red shirt she was wearing brought out the broken capillaries in her cheeks. "Did you get my flight details?"

He had and promptly informed her that a first-class ticket to Bombay would be waiting at the Pan-Asian Airlines counter at LAX, as well as a car when she arrived in Bombay to take her to a five-star hotel. All courtesy of Randy Kapoor.

"Fabulous," Raveena said and gave Griffin her parents' fax number so he could send over all the details.

She was about to go back inside when her call-waiting

beeped. Griffin was eager to get off the phone anyway and show off his new cashmere sweater, so she pressed the green call button. "Hello?"

"I have a date tomorrow night," Maza said.

This was interesting. Maza's dating life fascinated Raveena (and not just because Raveena didn't have one). Maza's last date had been with a shaman from the Arapaho tribe. Propping her elbows on her knees, she settled in for some juicy details. "Do divulge. Who's the man?"

"My gynecologist, Dr. Kim."

Raveena sat straight up. "What?"

"I was on the examining table when he asked if I was free this weekend."

"Your gyno! Isn't that against the law or something?"

She could hear Maza taking a drag of her cigarette.

"All his patients are women. He'd be crazy not to take advantage of the fact."

Raveena frowned. "I'm definitely not okay with this, Maza. The voodoo priest was weird enough, but this—"

"Listen," Maza interrupted. "Dr. Kim knows I'm free of disease. Beats hooking up at a bar or a club."

Raveena rubbed her forehead. "Remind me. You were spread-eagle at the time, right?"

This time when her call-waiting beeped she eagerly took the call. "Hello?"

"Hey," Jai said, distinctly morose.

"What's the matter?"

"Luke dumped me."

Luke was Jai's current flame. Raveena didn't care for the guy. Luke was from Long Beach but affected a stupid European accent and insisted on leaving wet slobbery kisses on both her cheeks as greetings. But Jai adored him, and she was sorry to hear the news. "Why? What happened?"

Jai had gone from morose to despondent. "He said I'm too gay."

"What?"

"I'm too gay for him," Jai said loudly.

Raveena was confused. Sure, Jai had less body hair than she, along with a flatter stomach and tighter ass, but those qualities were common in the gay community. "I don't understand; isn't Luke gay?"

Jai sounded exasperated. "Obviously."

Okay, this was too much.

Raveena was leaving for India in a few days. She didn't have time to deal with the dating dilemmas of her friends.

She did, however, agree to meet them for drinks that night at the Viceroy.

For a moment it felt good to be single.

The moment faded.

She shook her head and got up to go back inside.

Okay, seriously—back to the more important question.

What the hell was the deal with water in India anyway?

Chapter 7

*Raveena was standing in the first-class passenger line at the Pan-*Asian Airlines counter when she heard the horrible news.

The airline representative frowned at the computer and shook her head. "I'm sorry, but we don't have you on our first-class passenger list, Ms. Rai."

Raveena's stomach flipped and then flopped.

How could this be? She had the fax from Griffin in her hand.

Thanks to her mother—packer extraordinaire—she'd been able to fit into two suitcases what mere mortals could only hope to fit in seven. It had taken the combined efforts of her father, Jai and herself to heft each bag onto the weigh-in counter. All around her, Indian families were doing the same thing, paying overweight baggage fees, lugging their suitcases like oxen with a plow.

Raveena briefly wondered how the plane could possibly take off with all that extra weight.

But now . . .

Had Randy forgotten to get her ticket? Had Griffin gotten the dates wrong? Would her father be able to lug the suitcases back to their car without having a stroke?

Speaking of Bob, Raveena rubbed her aching right arm where she'd been poked and prodded by needles in preparation for the onslaught on her immune system in India. Daddy Dearest—having put the fear of God and hepatitis B in her—had begun clipping out articles about various disease epidemics in India and then calling and reading said articles to his daughter before she went off to sleep.

This did not provide for pleasant dreams.

When he clipped out an article about a possible typhoid scare in a town hundreds of miles from Bombay, Raveena's mother had finally taken away his scissors and forbade him to cut out another newspaper article for at least a year.

To make matters more complicated, Raveena's condo was now occupied by Jai, who, desperate to move out of his parents' home in Pasadena, had already shifted his things into her place and promised to take care of her plants.

Was it all for naught?

She forced herself to calm down. "Please check again. I know I'm leaving on this flight."

The clerk rubbed her chin and her fingers began flying over the keyboard. "Aha." She smiled and nodded. "I see what happened. You're definitely on the flight, Ms. Rai. Sorry about the mix-up."

Raveena relaxed and smiled back. "No problem. Once I'm in my seat with a glass of champagne in my hand, I'll forget this ever happened."

The clerk tapped her nose. "Hmm, well, you see, that's

sort of the mix-up. You're booked on the flight, but not in first class."

Raveena's mouth went dry. "What? Are you sure?"

The clerk tapped her nose again and nodded.

The woman really couldn't keep her hands off her face.

Raveena swallowed, and when she spoke, her voice was weak. "Business?"

The clerk frowned and shook her head no. "I'm sorry."

"You don't mean . . ."

The woman pinched the space between her eyes. "Yes, I'm afraid it's true."

Raveena's heart began pounding. A scream welled up in her throat.

The clerk gazed at her sympathetically. "You're booked in coach."

Raveena held onto the counter as the room swayed and dipped around her. She struggled to take a deep breath. So she'd be spending the next twenty-three hours in economy class.

That wasn't so bad, right?

Who was she kidding?

She'd rather date Maza's gynecologist.

"Isn't there something called economy class syndrome?" Raveena whispered.

The clerk tugged on her lower lip. "Yeah, you might want to walk up and down the aisle and stretch your legs at least every hour. Prevents a blood clot from forming."

She then pushed a button, printed out Raveena's boarding pass and handed it to her with a smile. "Enjoy your flight with Pan-Asian Airlines."

* * *

Bob wouldn't stop crying.

They were standing near the security checkpoint and Raveena's parents and friends could go no further.

Her father continued to cry.

Frankly, Raveena was a bit surprised.

Sure, she'd seen her father tear up before. He'd bawled in the theater during *The Joy Luck Club*. He'd bawled when his internist had informed him he had irritable bowel syndrome and not heart disease. He'd bawled when they'd gone to see Yo-Yo Ma in concert at the Dorothy Chandler Pavilion.

But he hadn't bawled when his parents had passed away. He didn't bawl—according to her mother—when Rahul and Raveena were born. And he'd never bawled during any of their family arguments, where Raveena struggled to act like an adult and usually ended up crying and losing all credibility.

But he was bawling now.

She hugged him. "It's okay, Dad. We'll be in touch. And I'm coming back."

"We'll miss you," he choked out between sobs.

Raveena looked over at her mother. Leela's eyes were bright but her lips were pressed in a straight line.

Her mother never wept.

Raveena pulled her mother into a hug.

Leela gently touched her daughter's hair. "Be safe," she whispered.

Jai looked like he was close to tears while Maza, like Raveena's mother, remained stoic.

And women were supposed to be too emotional?

From his pocket, her father pulled a handkerchief, dark blue this time, and mopped his face.

Raveena decided to end the good-byes before this turned into a wake.

She hugged Jai, who promised to ensure the survival of her leafy friends, and then hugged Maza last. Maza wasn't much of a hugger. Raveena loved her dearly but was positive there were corpses more affectionate.

"Here," Maza said and handed her a gift-wrapped present. "You'll need this in Bombay."

It looked too small to be a water-filtration system. In fact, it looked very much like a book.

And then Raveena was through the line and waving good-bye. Rahul had called the night before to wish her bon voyage.

Six months.

Raveena was starting to get *vaclempt*. Clutching the gift to her chest, she hoisted her shoulder bag and went through the security line. By the time she reached the end, her loved ones were no longer in view.

Taking a deep breath, Raveena headed for her boarding gate.

Chapter 8

Halfway through dinner, Randy Kapoor fired his screenwriter.

The man was in his mid-fifties with graying hair. He clutched the bound script to his chest and looked aghast.

"But I need this job. No one hires writers my age anymore."

"That's your problem," Randy said, as his mother entered the room and took a seat next to her son.

"Is the food to your liking?" his mother asked with a doting look, ignoring the older gentleman who continued to stand there with a helpless expression.

Randy pouted. "It's become cold."

His mother frowned. "Munnu! Come out here at once!"

Munnu, the household servant, appeared in the doorway. "Yes, memsahib."

"I told you Randy likes his food piping hot. Now, refill his plate and heat it up again."

Munnu stomped in, grabbed the plate and stomped back out.

"I don't like him, Mama," Randy fussed. "Munnu has a very bad attitude."

"Mr. Kapoor—" the screenwriter began with a beseeching look.

"Why are you still here?" Randy demanded.

Randy's mother stroked her son's arm soothingly, while shooting the screenwriter a dirty look. "You're aggravating my son during his dinner hour. It will give him indigestion." She turned back to Randy. "Don't worry about anything, my sweet. You're a growing boy. I'll tell Munnu to add another serving to your plate."

The fact was, Randy was a thirty-year-old man and had consumed half a pizza prior to dinner. In the last year, his waist size had expanded to a forty-two.

The screenwriter softly cleared his throat after Mrs. Kapoor had left the room. "But your father loved the script. He approved it. He thought the romance between the tour guide and the girl—"

"Daddy is not the director. I am," Randy informed him. "Your script was all about feelings and relationships. Boring. No fight scenes. No action. No explosions or skimpy costumes."

Munnu placed a plate laden with food in front of Randy.

"Munnu," Randy said, "show the man out."

Munnu dragged his feet over to the screenwriter and began urging him towards the door.

Happily, Randy dug into his food. He would write the script himself. How hard could it be?

A moment later his scream echoed throughout the house.

Mrs. Kapoor came running into the room, her massive bosom heaving underneath her sari blouse. "What is it, my sweet? What's wrong?"

"My food is too hot," Randy cried.

* * *

The driver quickly opened the back door of the green BMW. Randy slid into the leather seat and lit a cigarette. "Take me to Rain," he ordered the driver.

Rain was one of the hottest nightclubs in the city. Randy had just left a private party but wasn't in the mood to go home just yet.

The driver gazed at him in the rearview mirror. "But sahib, it's almost three A.M. Couldn't we head to the airport?"

Randy flicked the ash out the window and frowned. "Airport? Why would we go there?"

"Earlier you told me a woman would be arriving—"

"Stop making up stories," Randy said crossly through a haze of smoke. "Just drive."

There was more drinking to be done.

Chapter 9

Four A.M. outside Bombay's Sahar Airport.

The humidity was so thick you could hack it to pieces with a machete. Raveena waited for the promised car and driver to take her to the hotel.

And waited.

And waited some more.

And—just because it was so much fun—she kept on waiting.

It was twenty-three hours later, her eyes were gritty with lack of sleep, her stomach sour with airplane food, and her back hurt from the stiff seat—the middle seat, mind you—in a five-seat row.

Immediately after takeoff from LAX, the cute guy to her left had given her a cursory look, then turned to the petite blonde next to him and began chatting. Halfway into the flight they were making out like horny men in a Turkish prison. Raveena's polite "excuse me" was ignored.

The woman to her right had immediately taken half a

bottle of sleeping pills, followed by a double whiskey chaser, and conked out. This meant Raveena had to climb over her and the equally zonked Chinese gentleman in the aisle seat whenever she wanted to use the restroom.

Without a doubt, the airplane lavatory probably reeked worse than one of the port-a-potties at Woodstock 2, and Raveena thought of just holding it until the layover.

But her bladder had a mind of its own.

To make matters worse, during the four-hour layover in Singapore, she'd been cornered by a group of teenage Asian girls with matching backpacks shouting "Vagitsu! Vagitsu!" Disheveled as Raveena was, she'd agreed to pose in photographs and sign autographs.

"Ow!"

Raveena screeched as an Indian woman trod heavily on her foot.

The woman was unapologetic.

With her two enormously heavy suitcases beside her—honestly, it was as though she'd packed a sumo wrestler in each of them—her carry-on bag slowly cutting off the circulation of blood to her shoulder, her purse clutched to her chest in a death grip—Auntie Kiran had said India was filled with thieves and rapists—Raveena was jostled and pushed by the flood of humanity exiting Arrivals.

The buzzing sodium lights outside the airport bathed her skin in a strange orange hue and irritated her eyes. Beggars of all shapes and sizes, some with missing limbs, some with extra limbs—one man kept showing Raveena the third nostril on his nose—clamored for attention, their hands outstretched, their voices pleading. Hawkers battled with the beggars, waving worn and used-looking maps of Bombay, suspicious-looking bottled water and dented Bollywood film magazines.

The noise was intense and grating. She'd never experienced anything like it.

Taxi drivers cued up at the curb, competing with each other for passengers. Several of them kept opening their doors and trying to tempt her in.

And then there were the loafers. Auntie Kiran had warned Raveena about them.

The loafers were men who didn't seem to have any purpose but to lean against the wall and stare at each and every woman who crossed their field of vision. Since Raveena was the only unaccompanied female standing there, she was the sole object of their gaze.

Dressed in threadbare cotton clothing, they stared at her with bloodshot eyes, their feet bare, black hair oily. A few of them made smooching noises, which she wisely did not return.

And Raveena kept on waiting.

She had the fax from Griffin, which listed the name of the hotel, as well as Randy Kapoor's number, but she didn't have a cell phone on her, and the pay phones were on the opposite end of the crowded walkway. No way would she be able to lug her suitcases that far, and no way in hell was she leaving them unattended. The coolie who had carried her bags outside had long since disappeared into the night.

Besides, she'd passed by several pay phones after emerging from customs and they looked more complicated than *The Da Vinci Code.*

And she didn't have any Indian coins.

As five a.m. approached, having grown weary of the beggars, hawkers and loafers around her, Raveena finally grabbed a tall, gray-haired Indian gentleman who had just finished making a call on his cell phone. "Please, can you dial a number for me? My ride hasn't shown up."

He nodded and dialed the number she gave him. After a moment he handed it over. "It's ringing."

Raveena pressed the receiver to her ear as the phone rang and rang. Finally a sleepy and sullen male voice answered rudely in Hindi. "What."

She asked for Randy Kapoor.

The voice grew even more sullen. "Who?"

"Randy Kapoor."

"Kapoor sahib isn't here."

Damn. "Where is he? He was supposed to send the driver. I'm at the airport."

The man, whom she cleverly deduced to be the servant, repeated himself. "Kapoor Sahib isn't here."

She tried again. "Can you give me his cell number?"

The servant said something distinctly rude and untranslatable before hanging up.

"He's not there," Raveena said as she handed the phone back. Her mouth was suddenly dry and her palms sweaty. She was entering panic mode.

"Do you have his address?"

She dug the fax out of her bag and showed it to him. "No, but I have the hotel name."

The gentleman nodded and gestured for one of the taxi drivers to come over. In rapid Hindi he gave the man the hotel address and issued a stern warning to see Raveena there safely and promptly. The man nodded and went to pick up the suitcases.

Raveena turned to the gentleman, the sheer feeling of gratefulness nearly overwhelming her. "I can't thank you enough."

Her guardian angel smiled. "I have a daughter your age. I hope someone would do the same for her if she were stranded in a foreign city."

The taxi driver started the car; the gentleman held open the door and Raveena slid into the backseat.

Feeling like Blanche Dubois, she waved to her kind stranger as the car pulled away from the curb and plunged into the darkened bumpy streets of Bombay.

Twenty minutes later they pulled up in front of a sagging two-story building right on Juhu beach. A tarnished and rusted sign read:

Officer's Club

The taxi driver jumped out and began removing the suitcases from the car and dragging them to the entrance. Raveena stared at the forlorn empty drive covered with weeds. The windows on either side of the main door were cracked.

Maybe she was being a snob, but in her opinion, five-star accommodations did not mean a decrepit old building that had obviously seen its heyday during the British Empire.

Stunned, she stepped out and faced the driver. "My hotel?" He smiled and nodded. "Yes, madam."

Still in a daze, she paid him, walked up to the Officer's

Club door and opened it. A middle-aged man was asleep at the front desk.

"Excuse me," Raveena said loudly.

The night porter opened his eyes, blinked and rubbed his face.

"Do you have a reservation for Raveena Rai?"

He came over and handed her a large brass key, with a tag attached. "Room fifteen," he said. And then pointed at the stairs. "Up."

After that he went back to the front desk and was soon snoring away.

She stood there for a moment in the hall, as if in a trance.

Then she went back for her suitcases and managed to push them both inside, and then, alternately pushing and pulling one, struggled to get them upstairs.

Finally, soaked in sweat and nearly falling with exhaustion, she unlocked the door to number fifteen and stepped inside.

One small room. One thin cot. One solitary bulb in the ceiling.

She opened the bathroom door. A cracked, rusting porcelain toilet. The showerhead hung from the middle of the ceiling. There was a small drain in the floor.

The Ritz it wasn't.

Raveena closed and locked the room door, stumbled over to the cot and threw herself across it.

And there, in her small smelly quarters, mosquitoes hovering in wait, she cried herself to sleep.

Chapter 10

"I don't want to do this film," Siddharth said, *his voice flat.*

His manager, Javed Khan, sighed. "I agree with you, Sid. Randy Kapoor is a bastard of the first degree, and I wouldn't trust him alone in a room with a female goat, but Daddy asked for you personally."

"Daddy?" Siddharth could feel his resistance crumbling and cursed his luck at being born in July. He was a Cancer, which meant he was moody, sensitive and often wracked by guilt.

Damn those astrologers, they really got it right sometimes.

The last thing he wanted to do was work with a *chutia* like Randy Kapoor, but Randy's father and Daddy had been good friends. If he said no, every time he passed by his father's picture, framed by a garland of marigolds, he would feel guilty.

Then again, one romantic role was the same as another. The familiar feeling of boredom began creeping up on him. He sighed and slumped in his chair. "Who's the actress?"

His manager smiled approvingly and slid over a slim

Bollywood CONFIDENTIAL

portfolio case. "She's Indian, American born, from Los Angeles. Randy spied her in a commercial in Singapore."

Siddharth opened the portfolio and stared at the glossy eight-by-elevens.

The woman was beautiful; no doubt about that.

Her long black hair hung to the middle of her back. She had a sensuous quality, evident in her deep brown eyes and the slight curl of her full lips.

He noticed something in the last photo. "She has big feet."

Javed looked over. "She does, doesn't she? Her shoe size must be close to mine."

Siddharth shut the portfolio and sat back. "I've already committed to *Love in the Himalayas*. What about that?"

"No problem," Javed said. "I've looked at the dates. They won't overlap with Randy Kapoor's film."

Siddharth stood up, wearing a distinctly grumpy expression. "Fine. But I'm only doing this because Daddy asked."

His manager nodded. "I know, Sid." He reached for the phone and began dialing. "Will I see you tonight at the premiere for *Love along the Ganges*?"

Siddharth paused, his hand on the door. "Damn. I'd forgotten about that."

Emitting a string of Hindi obscenities that caused Javed to smile, Siddharth slipped on a pair of Revo sunglasses and was out the door.

Emitting a string of Hindi obscenities that caused Javed to smile, Siddharth slipped on a pair of Revo sunglasses and was out the door.

Chapter 11

The heat was so intense Raveena could practically hear the oil on her T-zone sizzling.

She was attempting to place an international call to Griffin back in Los Angeles. She had some specific words to say about Randy Kapoor.

That morning, a different—but equally sleepy—porter had been behind the front desk when she came downstairs. She'd barely slept five hours.

The porter had made no mention of the mosquito bites disfiguring her face, or how her eyes were swollen from crying.

When she'd asked about calling America—there was no telephone in her room—the porter pointed out the door, "Left, madam."

The sun beating down fiercely, she'd walked past carts selling coconut water, vendors frying up chickpeas and serving them in newspapers, and beggar women with naked children clinging to the skirts of their saris.

And the noise:

Horns blaring from cars and taxis, the roadrunner-like "beep, beep" from the black and yellow motorcycle rickshaws, known as auto-rickshaws, that buzzed down the street like angry hornets, the blasting of Bollywood hits from every stand, the barking of stray dogs as they chased one another alongside the road.

And the people:

Men and women on bicycles, on foot, in cars, in auto-rickshaws, in double-decker buses that looked as though they would topple over at any second with the number of people hanging out of windows and clinging onto the sides.

And everywhere she looked there were billboards advertising Coca-Cola, Pepsi, McDonalds, Omega Watches, MTV Asia, Sony electronics, the latest film release . . . a veritable attack of information.

Next to Bombay, Los Angeles suddenly seemed like a quaint New England village.

As a child, Raveena had accompanied her parents on several visits to India to see grandparents and various relatives. They'd arrive in New Delhi, be whisked off to the train station and travel first class to the northern town of Amritsar where both her parents had grown up.

But Bombay—

Bombay was something else.

What on earth had made her think she could handle it?

With the telephone stand's operator helping, she dialed the country code, then the area code and finally the number of Griffin's cell phone.

Groggily guessing, she figured it to be around nine-thirty in the evening in LA.

The phone continued to ring. If she got Griffin's voice mail she would become hysterical.

Raveena gave herself permission.

Fortunately for the telephone operator and anyone within screaming distance, Griffin answered.

"Hello?" he said.

"Griffin! This is Raveena!" she shouted.

"Raveena," he said in a casual voice. "How are you, doll? Did you make it all right? Can I put you on hold? I've got another call coming in."

She gritted her teeth. "Griffin I'm calling from thirteen thousand miles away. I know because I counted the fucking miles while on the plane. And if you dare put me on hold I will tell everyone about your butt implants."

That got his attention.

"Raveena, wow, you sound upset. What's up, babe?"

"That bastard Randy Kapoor flew me coach to India. There was no driver to meet me when I landed at four in the morning. And the five-star hotel? It's some sort of run-down military club. The toilet doesn't work. The shower is a drain in the middle of the floor. The bed has probably ruined my posture permanently, and I've got mosquitoes binging and purging on my face. You have to do something!"

She could practically hear Griffin rubbing his chin. "Hmm. Well that's not what Randy promised at all. I'm sure it's a misunderstanding, doll. Call me back in an hour."

And then he hung up.

Raveena knew there was no misunderstanding. She'd seen the same type of behavior in some of her Indian relatives, especially in the wealthier ones.

Randy Kapoor was a cheap asshole.

For a while, she waited outside the telephone stand. She was drenched in so much sweat she could have started a salt factory then and there. She hadn't eaten anything, her stomach was upset, and she wasn't a big fan of coconut water or fried chickpeas.

The loafers loafing about stared, and she stared back at them angrily. Auntie Kiran had told her to ignore them, but she was in no mood to be docile. If even one of them dared make a smooching noise . . .

Finally, she became so thirsty she decided to walk down to a small roadside stand and buy a soda. They were out of Coke and Pepsi but an Indian cola called Thums Up was in stock. It was cold, and that was all she cared about. After a few tentative sips she found herself liking it. It was on the sweeter side like Pepsi but had sort of a spicy aftertaste.

Raveena blessed her mother for having the foresight to give her a bundle of rupees left over from numerous trips to India. She was in no mood to search for an Indian ATM.

Finishing her drink, she wiped her mouth with the back of her hand and returned the empty glass bottle to the clerk. She then emitted a very unladylike belch. No one paid any mind, and her stomach instantly felt better.

Raveena was about to walk away when she noticed a boy and girl sitting next to each other in the shade. Their dusty faces and bare feet betrayed their economic status.

She bought them each a Thums Up and two bags of masala-flavored Ruffles potato chips. In return, the kids rewarded her with big smiles, their teeth surprisingly white and perfect.

Raveena walked back to the phone stand and waited. Only fifty minutes had passed, but she wasn't about to twiddle her thumbs or stare at the cow lounging on the road just to kill ten more minutes.

So she called Griffin back.

For the first time, Griffin answered the phone without enthusiasm. His "hey, doll" was almost apologetic.

This was bad.

"Tell me," Raveena said.

"Randy is definitely not being cool. He refuses to pay for alternate accommodations. He also said he needed to make use of his car and driver last night, and that's why they couldn't meet you."

"And what about the promised first-class ticket?" she demanded.

"He said that by first class he meant traveling by plane, not a first-class plane ticket."

"What was the alternative? Traveling by steamship?"

Griffin sighed. "I don't know what to tell you, doll. Your role is legit, though. You will be playing the heroine of Randy's film. I have the contract to back that up. But I do have some good news."

Quentin Tarantino had written a role for a belly-dancing assassin in his new movie, and she'd be perfect for it.

The heat was obviously making her delusional.

"Yes?" she asked.

"I spoke with your mother."

"Mom?"

"She says you have a distant uncle who lives in Bombay. She's contacted him, and he's agreed to let you stay with him for the duration of the filming."

Distant uncle was right. Raveena knew that her mother's cousin's wife's nephew's grandmother had a brother who lived in Bombay. Leela had given her his address and phone number and ordered her to visit or at least call him while she was there. Apparently he was in his sixties and lived alone. Although she hadn't seen her uncle in thirty years, Leela dutifully sent him a card every Indian New Year.

"Stay with an uncle I've never met?" Raveena questioned weakly.

"I'm sorry, doll. Either stay put or head to your uncle's. Otherwise you can come back to LA. A role came across my desk this morning. They need someone to play Sacajawea's sister in a made-for-TV movie about Lewis and Clark. They've got the kid from *Small Wonder* playing Sacajawea. The sister doesn't have any dialogue but . . ." his voice trailed off.

Raveena closed her eyes and leaned her head against the booth. Then she opened her eyes and nearly screamed when she saw the dead fly guts sprayed all over the glass. She screamed again and wiped her forehead.

What should she do?

Part of her longed to go back to LA. Her spirit of adventure had been replaced with fear, anxiety, self-doubt and resentment.

Plus, she missed her mommy and daddy.

Maybe she'd go back, land the role of Sacajawea's sister, and finally be noticed.

Right.

That was about as far-fetched as her curling up alongside the cow for a snooze on the road.

She'd come this far. This was still her best break. She thought of Anthony Quinn and took a deep breath. "I'm staying, Griffin. I'll move in with my uncle."

"Excellent." Griffin sounded relieved. "Do you have the address?"

Raveena took out a piece of paper from her bag.

Heeru Punjabi
17 Portugal Road
Bandra
Bombay

It was time to meet the distant uncle she'd be spending the next six months of her life living with.

She wondered if he had a liquor cabinet.

Chapter 12

Raveena had never checked out of a place as fast as she did from the odious Officer's Club.

In a burst of strength—she was channeling Bionic Woman—she grabbed a suitcase in each hand and dragged them down the stairs running, knocking the porter down in the process.

Once outside, she waited impatiently as the taxi driver struggled to fit her bags in the trunk. Finally, she elbowed him out of the way and did it herself.

And then with a resounding slam of the car doors, they sped away in a cloud of dust.

Uncle Heeru lived in a suburb of Bombay known as Bandra.

Bombay was divided into two sections: South Bombay, or the city, and the outlying northern suburbs. Bandra was the suburb closest to the city. Raveena knew this because she'd purchased the *Lonely Planet Guide to India* at Barnes & Noble before she left.

They drove along Turner Road, the busy Bandra thoroughfare, and then headed away from the shop-lined streets and tall buildings housing expensive flats.

They passed Catholic churches—Bandra had a large Indian Christian community—and veered towards the ocean, making a right along the famous Bandra Bandstand. According to the guidebook, at sunset the Bandstand would turn into a veritable lover's paradise, with couples strolling hand in hand and venturing out onto the rocks to sit and be alone.

And then they were turning away from the water and heading up a winding street. The thick growth of trees on either side blissfully blocked out the unrelenting sun.

Between the trees, Raveena could see mountain cabin-like duplexes and stunning gated villas. She felt her spirits rise. Maybe staying with her uncle wouldn't be so bad.

The driver had to stop and ask directions three times because none of the homes seemed to have numbers on them. After the third set of directions, the driver drove a few more meters, stopped short, made a sharp right and plunged down a dusty wooded drive.

He cut the engine.

They'd arrived.

Raveena looked out the window at her new abode and her mouth dropped open.

She quickly closed it because she didn't want to look slow.

In front of her was a two-story faded gray bungalow that desperately needed an HGTV makeover. A wide wraparound porch encircled the house. The area around the bungalow was dark and heavily wooded with red oak, palm and mango trees. Hawks circled above and she could hear the cawing of hundreds of crows.

She paid the taxi driver, then went up three short steps and knocked on the heavy wooden door.

She had no idea what to expect, and *Lonely Planet* didn't have any answers.

Chapter 13

From his second-floor bedroom, Heeru Punjabi watched the young woman exit the taxi.

This must be the niece from America, he thought. The one who was an actress. What was her name? Lavinia something or the other?

Heeru shook his head. What was she doing acting in a Bollywood film? Everyone knew the industry was a terrible place. Any decent young woman would refuse to work there.

Heeru knew either Nandini or Nanda, the two young sisters he employed as servants, would see to the guest, so he stayed in his room sprinkling bird feed onto the floor and along the windowsill. He considered all winged creatures godlike. Even if they did seem to defecate frequently on his head with abandon.

Heeru did not want this American niece of his staying with him. He did not like visitors. However, if he refused her room and board he would most likely return in his next life as a lizard of some sort.

Several gray pigeons and one pushy black one flew in and began pecking at the seed.

Yes, the film industry was a wicked place, and Heeru should know. He had once dreamt of becoming an actor.

Heeru continued to sprinkle seed and thought back to the year 1962.

The sixth of eight children, eighteen-year-old Heeru knew from careful study that he was the best looking of all of them. His four sisters had unfortunately inherited their mother's propensity to put on weight and their father's bulbous nose—which some had likened to a hard plum after the crows had picked at it.

Heeru and his three brothers were all slim like their father, but his eldest brother Arjun had already begun to lose his hair. Nanu, Heeru's younger brother and the smartest of all the siblings—the school principal's opinion, not Heeru's—was favored with a fair complexion and hazel eyes, but had no dress sense or style—Heeru's opinion, not the school principal's.

The remaining brother Jagdish was a lout, and Heeru's mother blessed the day he had moved to Hong Kong to seek his fortune.

Definitely, Heeru was the only one with the potential to make it as an actor. Admittedly, he could have done with a fair complexion like Nanu's—instead his skin was the color of toffee—but Heeru kept it glowing and radiant with nightly applications of his mother's herbal face tonic. The tonic was expensive, and Heeru had to wait until his mother was asleep before sidling into her room and slipping the small bottle off her dresser.

Basically, Heeru was all set to pursue his dream of a career under the lights when something happened.

The incident involved the park where Heeru "rehearsed." He regularly took the bus to a secluded park where he could practice being a film hero. He didn't even consider practicing at home in his room, not with four prying plum-nosed sisters around. There in the park among the poplar trees he could rehearse in peace.

Heeru always wore the same outfit on these occasions. In his white slacks, matching jacket, red silk shirt and paisley scarf knotted dashingly around his neck, Heeru knew he cut a fine figure.

Then, with one arm around the tree trunk—pretending it was the ample waist of a lotus-eyed actress, Heeru would croon the latest melody, crinkling his eyes, moving his brows up and down and flipping the puff in his hair just like the latest heartthrob.

But then one day a group of young ruffians from the lowest rung of the caste ladder came upon Heeru embracing a tree and burst into loud laughter. They also made lewd gestures and called Heeru names, comparing him to mediocre actors he couldn't stand.

Heeru was tempted to yell and remind them of their class, but his legs had a mind of their own, and he turned tail and ran. The youths, sensing some fun in their unemployed, poverty-stricken lives, decided to give chase.

Heeru ran and ran. He tripped and fell a few times, sobbing like any heroine in a chase scene running to save her virtue. By the time he climbed aboard the bus and dropped into his seat shaking, his favorite slacks were torn and covered with grass stains. He touched his neck and realized his paisley scarf was gone.

Heeru never rehearsed again.

For a moment, awash in the old memory, he looked wildly around, but the room was occupied only by pigeons, one of which was currently using his shoe as a toilet.

Chapter 14

Raveena followed a slender, dark-skinned young woman with a shy smile into the sitting room.

The young woman was dressed in a cotton housecoat with short sleeves. Her feet were bare. She indicated Raveena should take a seat and then disappeared into another room.

Raveena sat down on a lumpy white sofa, immediately sinking deep into the cushions. Directly above her were two ceiling fans. It was stuffy and muggy in the room, so she flipped the wall switch and the blades sprang to life on the fastest setting. Her long hair whirled around her face and the stack of newspapers on the coffee table blew across the room. Quickly, she flipped the switch back down, retrieved the newspapers and tried to smooth down her hair.

The young woman returned with a tall glass of water. "Safe," she began and her smooth brow furrowed. Then with another shy smile she pointed at the glass and said, "Filtered." Only, the way she said it made the word sound like "pilltered."

Absolutely charmed by her sweet demeanor, Raveena accepted the glass of water. "Thank you." The water was cold, and she practically downed the entire contents in one gulp.

The young woman smiled approvingly and disappeared again.

Raveena proceeded to sit alone in the room for the next twenty minutes.

Finally, she decided she may as well explore her new surroundings. In one corner of the room was a large wooden altar dominated by a white marble statue of Lord Ganesh, the remover of obstacles, along with small framed paintings of the Goddess Lakshmi and Lord Krishna. There was also a large photograph of a round-faced man with a black Afro dressed in an orange robe. She'd seen that same photograph in other Indian homes. The man was Sathya Sai Baba. She moved closer and saw there was a caption at the bottom of the photograph.

Hurt Never. Love Ever.

Made sense.

So Uncle Heeru was a Sai Baba devotee. From what she'd read, Sai Baba was considered an avatar of God. In front of eyewitnesses, he had raised the dead, materialized jewelry out of thin air, turned water into gasoline when his car ran out of fuel, made sweets appear directly into people's mouths and managed to appear in two places at once.

Further examination of the altar was halted when she looked up to see another girl, shorter and darker than the first but dressed almost identically in a short-sleeved housecoat, staring at her. Raveena smiled but was pointedly ignored. The girl's expression was decidedly sulky. Silently, she disappeared into another room and Raveena was once again left alone.

She returned to the sofa and stared at the large Toshiba television in the corner of the room. A black pigeon flew in through the open window, perched on the top of a bookcase and fixed its red gaze on her.

Raveena found this to be slightly unnerving and was about to get up and look for someone, anyone, when rapid footsteps sounded from the hall. All of a sudden a man came tearing into the room, stopped at the sight of her and ran his hands through his shock of thick white hair.

He was of average height, thin with a slight paunch, wore steel-rimmed glasses held together strategically with scotch tape and dressed in a faded white cotton shirt and what looked like a brand new pair of Levi's 501 jeans. The jeans were too long and his feet peeked out from beneath the cuffs in brown leather Kolhapuri slippers.

Raveena stood up. "Uncle Heeru?" she asked tentatively.

He ran his fingers through his hair again, causing it to stand up in tufts. "Yes, you're here," he said. "Nice, ah, to see you again."

"We've never met," Raveena said.

His eyes darted right and left. "Yes, that's right." All of a sudden he tipped his head back and shouted, "Nandini! Nanda!"

From another room a female voice yelled back, "What do you want?"

"See to the guest!"

The two servants, one smiling and the other sulky, came into the room.

"Show Lavinia to her room," Uncle Heeru said.

"It's Raveena. And I wanted to thank you so much for letting me stay here."

Uncle Heeru gazed at her blankly. She found this almost as unnerving as the pigeon.

"I just wanted to, umm, really thank you," she repeated lamely. "I promise I won't be any trouble. If I can be of help—"

"What is the time?" Uncle Heeru interrupted. Before anyone could answer he looked down at his bare wrist. "Where is my wristwatch? Thieves have stolen my wristwatch!"

"Nobody stole it; you lost it yourself months ago," the sulky servant said crossly.

"Never mind," Uncle Heeru said to no one in particular. "Nandini, take Lavinia to her room."

The young woman with the shy smile came forward and gestured towards the stairs.

So this was Nandini. Raveena definitely liked her.

The other girl—Nanda—continued to stand there, her arms crossed over her chest.

"Go find Chotu and tell him to bring in the suitcases," Uncle Heeru said to her.

Nanda frowned and fired back in rapid Hindi Raveena could barely follow. Something about Chotu stealing a potato.

This caused Uncle Heeru to pull on his hair, yell, and then run out of the room, his slippers clopping on the cement floor.

Nanda sniffed and turned away, skirt swirling.

Raveena followed Nandini up the stairs and into what would be her bedroom.

It was a large space. A double bed was covered in a pretty, red embroidered bedcover. Directly above it a ceiling fan slowly circulated the heavy humid air. Across from the bed was a window that ran the entire length of the wall. It was screenless, shutterless and, Raveena realized, pigeon-accessible. It was also facing the sun, which meant sleeping in would be difficult. The walls were bare except for a Sathya Sai Baba calendar. The orange-robed man held his hand up in blessing.

Nandini crossed the room and opened the double doors of an ancient Godrej wardrobe. Raveena's mother had had one just like it in India. Smiling, Nandini gestured towards the empty shelves. Raveena smiled back and nodded. Nandini then crossed to a door Raveena hadn't seen. It led to a small guest bathroom.

Raveena was pleased to see the toilet was sparkling clean. There was a mirrored cabinet for her toiletries and an enormous green marble bathtub big enough for two people. Raveena was more of a shower person, but the bathtub looked fun. Not that she'd be doing any entertaining in it.

Raveena thanked Nandini and drifted towards the window. Looking down she could see into the courtyard. A young man was struggling with her suitcases. Chotu, she presumed, and continued to watch as Uncle Heeru came running out of the house and started shouting. Chotu shouted back. Uncle Heeru pulled at his hair again and stomped his foot.

Raveena's mother had said something about the family regarding Heeru as a sort of swami.

If that were true—

He was the most stressed-out swami Raveena had ever met.

Chapter 15

The next morning Raveena was having breakfast alone when Randy Kapoor's secretary called.

Nanda brought her the phone and silently handed it over.

"Thank you," Raveena said.

Nanda's expression remained sulky.

Nandini was definitely preferable.

"Hello?"

"Good morning, ma'am, I'm calling from Mr. Kapoor's office. Mr. Kapoor would like you to meet him here at one P.M.," a woman said in precise Indian English.

No wonder outsourcing was going to India. The professionals here spoke better English than Raveena did.

"Okay," Raveena said. "The only thing is, I don't know where his office is."

"Yes, ma'am, I will give you the directions. Where exactly are you residing, ma'am?"

Since arriving in India she'd been called madam and ma'am more times than in her entire life put together.

"Umm, I'm in Bandra. Portugal Road."

"Very good, ma'am. A beautiful area. Our office is in Bandra as well."

"It is?"

"Yes, ma'am, Bandra is home to many producers, directors and stars. Now, tell the auto-rickshaw driver to take you to Turner Road and—"

"Auto-rickshaw?" Raveena interrupted. No way was she getting in one of those things. "I was planning on taking a taxi."

"Oh no, ma'am. A taxi will not take you such a short distance, and why pay extra money besides? Tell the auto-rickshaw driver to take you to Turner Road and from there 14th Road. We are located at 29 Jains Arcade, on the 2nd floor."

Raveena was scribbling this down as quickly as she could. "Jains Arcade. Got it."

"Wonderful. I will tell Mr. Kapoor to expect you at one. Have a nice day, ma'am."

Raveena set down the phone and ate some more of the scrambled eggs Nandini had made. They were delicious, flavored with green chilies, tomato and cumin.

Stuffed, she pushed the plate aside and a large black crow immediately swooped in through the dining room window and scooped the egg off her plate. She screamed and threw up her hands.

The crow then perched on the ledge of the window, gazed at Raveena with a beady eye and promptly guzzled the piece of egg.

Since yesterday, she'd been startled by all manner of winged creatures flying in and out of the house. Because of the heat and Uncle Heeru's devotion to birds, all the windows were open all the time. When she'd asked her uncle why he didn't invest in air-conditioning, he'd responded by saying he did not want to catch a cold.

The average temperature in Bombay that winter was eighty-eight degrees.

Earlier, Raveena had seen Uncle Heeru fighting with a crow over a piece of papaya.

With a sigh of acceptance, she pushed her plate closer to the window and addressed the crow. "Dig in."

Wings outstretched, the crow once more swooped in and grabbed the last piece of egg. Instead of dining on the ledge, the bird flew up into the trees shading the house.

American crows definitely had better manners.

Two hours later, Raveena thought she was going to die.

The auto-rickshaw darted in and out of traffic, at times jumping up on the walkway, before zooming back onto the street. Open on both sides without doors, the contraption made her feel exposed. And she was guaranteed maximum exposure to exhaust fumes.

Raveena had done her hair for the meeting, setting it with Velcro rollers, but the wind and humidity wreaked havoc with the curls. If she was going to be traveling by auto-rickshaw, she'd have to do it Jackie O. style, with a headscarf.

Then again, Raveena saw plenty of Muslim women in *burkhas* walking up and down the street and thought about wearing one herself for practical reasons. Her hair would be covered. Her face would be protected from grime, and she wouldn't have to worry about her clothes getting dirty.

The heat was relentless. Not wanting to arrive at the meeting with foundation melting off her face, she'd wisely kept the makeup to a minimum. Just some eyeliner and a dab of Chanel lipgloss.

However, Raveena was regretting her choice of clothing. Her parents had warned her to dress conservatively while in India. So she was wearing beige trousers and a white tailored Oxford shirt.

Meanwhile, right alongside the conservative Muslim women in *burkhas* were teenage girls in shorts and twenty-something women in tank tops, jeans and everything in between.

Obviously, Bombay was to India what Los Angeles was to the rest of America.

A whole different world.

Raveena especially liked the cute cotton tunics or *kurtas* she'd seen many women of all ages sporting. They looked comfortable and stylish. Raveena decided to buy half a dozen for Maza and herself while here.

"Fourteenth Road," the driver said, spitting a stream of tobacco juice into the gutter. He was thickset and heavy, sweat visibly seeping through his khaki-colored clothing.

"Okay," Raveena said, happy the tobacco spray had missed her nether regions. "29 Jains Arcade?"

The driver didn't reply, so she repeated the question. He gave her an impatient nod.

"Fine," she said, sat back and watched the scenery chug by. Cars, buses and auto-rickshaws battled each other for the road. Skinny cows walked alongside, nosing through rubbish for food. The barking of stray dogs was everywhere.

The driver stopped beside a small stand where a man was busy rolling bidis—cheap tapered cigarettes that looked like marijuana joints.

Not realizing they'd arrived at the place, Raveena continued to sit in the back of the rickshaw until the driver turned, looked at her and pointed to the right. She turned and saw a large building.

Raveena paid the driver twenty rupees, about forty cents, and very carefully crossed the street, dodging bicyclists, auto-rickshaws, cars and a hungry cow.

There was a guard at the entrance to the building who stopped her before she could go in. He had an AK-47 strapped to his back.

One of them was seriously packing too much metal.

"I'm here to see Randy Kapoor," she said, trying to look as non-threatening as possible.

The guard looked her up and down, decided she didn't pose a menace, and nodded. Raveena opened the door and nearly let out a sigh of relief as the air-conditioned coolness washed over her.

She took the elevator up to the second floor and found herself confronted by a set of thick glass double doors. Engraved into the glass were the words:

Karma Productions

Behind the glass she could see trendy twenty-something Indians walking back and forth, answering phones and working on computers. Raveena entered the bright purple and orange lobby—very MTV—and went up to the black circular front desk.

"I'm Raveena Rai, here to see Randy Kapoor."

"Oh, yes, Miss Rai," the woman smiled. "Please come with me."

Raveena followed her through another set of double doors and into a lavish waiting room done up in marble. Two beautiful gold statues of Lakshmi, the Goddess of Wealth, occupied alcoves on opposite walls. A second woman sitting behind a black marble desk rose at their entrance.

"Raveena?" the second woman asked, and Raveena recognized her voice from the phone that morning. The woman came forward smiling. "I'm Millie D'Souza."

Millie was petite, her black hair cut in a shiny bob. A slender gold cross gleamed against her throat. "Mr. Kapoor has yet to arrive. Can I get you some coffee? A cold drink?"

"I'd love something cold. Ah, you don't happen to have Thums Up, do you?" Raveena had been craving the drink since yesterday.

Millie looked surprised. "Yes, we do. It's my favorite, but most people prefer Coke or Pepsi."

Raveena took a seat on a plush burgundy sofa while Millie returned to her desk and pushed a button on the intercom.

A few moments later a young boy entered the room carefully balancing a tray with two tall glasses, his bare feet moving soundlessly across the floor.

Millie waited until he had left, then took a sip of her drink. "In America you do not have people like our office boys?"

Raveena thought about certain personal assistants in Hollywood who were expected not only to make calls, but wash the star's Chihuahua's butt, plan parties for the star's kids, arrange for sex escorts and bring coffee. But she knew what Millie meant.

"No, we don't. I mean, secretaries will make coffee for their bosses and get lunch, but that's not their main job. And they're usually eighteen years old and over."

Millie nodded.

Raveena sat back and drank her Thums Up. She was getting addicted to the stuff.

By the time she finished her drink, Randy still had not arrived. Millie was busy taking phone calls and working on the computer but would shoot Raveena sympathetic looks now and again.

To entertain herself, Raveena thumbed through several glossy Bollywood magazines. That was how she got two pieces of very bad news.

The first was from an article on, yes, Randy Kapoor. Apparently, his last five films had all been expensive flops. The very last had been a Bollywood rip-off of *Runaway Bride*.

She peered closely at a picture of a thin, balding gray-haired man in a suit. He was wiping his brow and looked like the worried accountant of a mobster. According to the caption, it was Randy Kapoor's financier and father, Daddy.

The picture of Randy himself was blurry, and she could barely make out his features. She did, however, make out the bright yellow Tommy Hillfiger jacket he was wearing.

Very Ali G.

The second piece of bad news was from the gossip pages of a Bollywood rag called *Stardust*. Raveena was shocked to see her name mentioned. Well, not her name per se, but it was pretty obvious who they were talking about. She quickly scanned the lines:

Rumors have it that casting couch Casanova Randy Kapoor has brought in a foreign actress to play the heroine in his next film. According to the copulating Kapoor, the role required someone of Indian origin but with an

American accent. However, *Stardust* tattlers tell the real
tale. As it turns out, no self-respecting Bombay actress
will work with the randy Randy. We wish the poor unsus-
pecting Yank all the best. Maybe she should have brought
a chaperone with her . . .

Great. Raveena had barely been in Bombay for two days,
and already her reputation was being battered and splat-
tered across the pages of India's answer to *Variety!*

About the randy Randy business—sure, the casting
couch was a fixture in Hollywood as well. But Raveena had
never encountered it.

She couldn't decide whether to be flattered or offended
about that.

Raveena was still deciding when the door opened and
Millie looked up. "Mr. Kapoor," she said.

Raveena put the magazines away and prepared herself.

She was finally going to meet Randy Kapoor.

Chapter 16

Not surprisingly, Raveena didn't care for the director.

And it wasn't because he grabbed her ass as soon as they entered his private office.

Randy Kapoor was, in the words of philosopher Thomas Hobbes, nasty, brutish and short.

"I consider myself the Quentin Tarantino of India," Randy said with a smug smile. "Or maybe a cross between Tarantino and Coppola." He laughed loudly.

Since Chris Rock wasn't in the room, Raveena didn't know what the hell was so funny.

Randy was about thirty, five-five and slightly on the chubby side. He was dressed head to toe in Polo Sport: Polo baseball cap, Polo sunglasses, Polo track pants and a Polo T-shirt.

Privately, she decided to refer to him as Mr. Polo Sport from now on.

Mr. Polo Sport didn't bring up the accommodations or her flight.

Instead, Randy fixed her with what he probably thought was a seductive smile.

Raveena thought he looked constipated.

"The moment I saw your ad in Singapore, I knew you were the one," he said. "You were very voluptuous and seductive."

"Err, thank you."

He leaned back in his chair. "My last film was nearly screened in Cannes. I suppose you saw it. It was a super hit."

"Oh, the remake of *Runaway Bride*?" Raveena asked.

Honestly, she said that without any sarcasm.

Randy narrowed his eyes. "My film was *inspired* by *Runaway Bride*. Why can't anyone see that?" He sat forward and stared directly at her. "Let me ask you a question. You don't hate the Japanese, do you?"

"Of course not!"

Randy threw out his hands. "Well, I'm like the Japanese; I take something American and make it better. Don't you use Japanese products? Well, that's me. I'm like Sony and Hollywood is Panasonic. We both exist in the same market." He sat back in his chair and beamed.

Raveena shifted in her chair, and for the umpteenth time since arriving at Randy's office, she questioned what the hell she was doing peddling her acting prowess in Bombay.

Oh right, because she didn't have any other offers.

To distract herself, Raveena checked out the office artwork and felt oddly comforted.

Glossy posters of sexy Bollywood heroines and studly Bollywood heroes in blockbuster Bollywood films graced the walls.

Movies starring people who looked just like her.

Okay, so maybe her boobs weren't as uplifting as the actress's in the poster to her right, and she'd yet to see an Indian guy who looked as good as the actor featured in the poster to her left . . .

And yet that wasn't the point.

The only Indian face Raveena had regularly seen on TV while growing up was Apu from *The Simpsons*.

God, how she loved Apu.

Randy interrupted her reverie. "I knew you would be perfect for my film."

No one had ever told Raveena she was perfect for a film.

Well, no one other than Griffin, and he was usually talking out of his ass.

She felt herself softening a bit towards the randy Randy.

Crossing her legs, Raveena flashed him a smile. "Well, considering your main character is a girl from America. I'd say I'm absolutely perfect."

"We're not doing *that* film any longer," Randy corrected.

Raveena sat forward. "Excuse me?"

"Romantic films are out." He waved his hand dismissively. "The audience wants action. They want lavish sets. They want larger than life."

She gripped the arms of her chair. "No one told me about this. Does my agent know? I was never sent a new script."

"There is no script as of yet," Randy said. "I'll begin working on one after we start shooting."

Did she just hear correctly?

Randy took note of her shocked look. "The story is the least important aspect of the film."

"Am I still the lead?"

Randy was about to say something when he paused, and

placed his hand on a piece of paper, pushing it towards her. "Confidentiality agreement. No word of my film can leave this room. If it does, I will have you before the Bombay High Court."

Randy Kapoor, who had remade *Runaway Bride* without permission, was afraid of someone stealing his idea?

Raveena grabbed the paper and signed her name with a flourish. "I'd like to hear about this new film now."

Randy framed his hands as though he were looking through a camera lens. "Picture the Taj Mahal. Who in the world has not heard of it? The Taj is a world wonder and synonymous with India."

Yeah, she'd read the guidebook and been there with her parents. "Go on."

"The epic of Shah Jahan and Mumtaz Mahal is a great love story. When Mumtaz died Shah Jahan threw himself into building the greatest testament to love the world has ever seen."

From what Raveena's dad—a history buff—had told her, Mumtaz Mahal had been a beautiful shy bride, gentle and sweet.

It wouldn't be that much of a stretch for Raveena to play her.

"So, I'm going to play Mumtaz Mahal?"

"Well," Randy hesitated, "my vision of her. I don't want to turn this into a romance."

He didn't want to turn the greatest love story ever told into a romantic movie? She waited for him to clarify.

"In my vision, Mumtaz Mahal is like Xena, the warrior princess. Xena was very popular in India. Instead of coming to Shah Jahan a shy bride, Mumtaz meets him on the battlefield where she defeats him in hand-to-hand combat. Eventually their hate turns to love. I plan to use Hong Kong–style action sequences."

Raveena could feel an ache building in her temples. "Let me get this straight. Mumtaz Mahal is now a warrior-princess who kicks the emperor's ass and then falls in love with him?"

Randy nodded excitedly.

The ache in her temples began to pound. "And what is this ah, movie, going to be called?"

Randy rubbed his hands gleefully. *"Taj Mahal 3000 . . . Unleashed!"*

Jesus Christ!

She needed some Advil.

Chapter 17

Half an hour later, Raveena found herself at Sahara Studios. She was sitting in the shade of a coconut tree drinking a Thums Up and waiting for the rest of the cast and crew to arrive.

She'd decided to be positive about *Taj Mahal 3000: Un-leashed.* It was her first shot at a leading role, and she was determined to throw herself whole-heartedly into the project.

Randy was pacing up and down the walkway blabbing into his cell phone.

Raveena took another swig and gazed around.

Sahara Studios was made up of a long dirt drive and several low-slung, one-story whitewashed buildings. Coconut trees were everywhere.

A door opened in one of the buildings, and a man walked towards them. She recognized him from his picture in the film magazine. The producer of the film.

Daddy.

Raveena didn't know whether it was the suit he wore that reminded her of her father or his gentle yet welcoming smile, but she instantly liked him.

"How are you *beti*?" he asked.

Beti was the Hindi word for daughter. Raveena was touched and liked him even more.

"I'm fine Mr. Kapoor. Thank you."

He shook his head. "No, you must call me Daddy. Everyone does."

"Okay . . . Daddy."

"Your accommodations are good?"

"Yes. I'm staying with my uncle."

For a moment he looked puzzled. "But I thought the Holiday Inn . . ." He shot a glance at Randy, who was still on his cell. Daddy turned back to her. "Never mind. It is always better to stay with family, no?"

Raveena was tempted to ask him about the Holiday Inn. Was that where Daddy had arranged for her to stay? Could she be basking in air-conditioned bliss instead of perspiring at Uncle Heeru's? She was about to open her mouth and tell Daddy all about how his son had booked a room at the Officer's Club instead, but then thought better of it.

Raveena would complain, and then Daddy would confront Randy. Randy would be on the defensive and probably take it out on her. He might even find some way to kick Raveena off his film.

She kept her mouth shut. After all, she'd be spending most of her time at the studio anyway.

Daddy took a seat in the lawn chair next to her as two cars pulled up and parked beside Randy's dark green BMW. A short, very fat man tumbled out of the first car, and a tall, rugged Sikh wearing cowboy boots and a turban exited the second.

Randy finally got off the phone. "Raveena," he said, "Let

me perform introductions." He gestured to the round man. "This is the choreographer, Lollipop. He'll handle all six song sequences."

Lollipop? Raveena struggled not to burst into giggles. As if sensing her amusement, Lollipop shot her a challenging look. She immediately sobered up.

Randy indicated the other man who lounged against the hood of his car. "This is Dharamveer Sandhu, the cinematographer."

Dharamveer lit up a cigarette. "Everyone calls me Veer."

"Veer is the best cinematographer in India," Randy boasted.

Instead of acknowledging the compliment, Veer blew out a perfect ring of smoke and ignored Randy completely.

"Where's Siddharth?" Lollipop asked in a high-pitched voice.

Raveena giggled. Everyone looked at her.

Struggling to contain herself, she cleared her throat. "Who's Siddharth?"

Lollipop turned towards Raveena in disbelief. "You don't know who Siddharth is?"

Veer looked at Daddy in surprise. "We have Siddharth? How did you manage that?"

"Oh, Siddharth and I are great friends," Randy said, butting in. "He's doing this as a personal favor to me."

Raveena was definitely intrigued. Siddharth hadn't starred in any of the Bollywood films she'd seen. Although, admittedly, the ones she'd borrowed had been a few years old.

"Will Siddharth be playing the Emperor then?" she asked.

Lollipop was practically jumping up and down. "I can't wait to work with Siddharth! The man moves like a dream!"

Veer flicked the ash from his cigarette and continued to muse. "We have Siddharth . . ."

Daddy answered Raveena's question. "Yes *beti*, Siddharth is the biggest star in India. We are very blessed to have him in our film."

"There he is!" Randy crowed, pointing to a black Mercedes pulling into the drive.

The windows were tinted, so Raveena couldn't get a look inside.

The car stopped, the driver side door opened, and it was as though time stood still.

Raveena was *so* not kidding.

Conversation ceased. Various men and women going about their own studio business moved closer and stared.

And no wonder.

Siddharth was the Adonis of the East.

He was around six feet tall, lean and muscled. His skin was a golden bronze and his hair a rich dark brown. He had that perfect Roman nose, and his eyes were hazel.

And if that weren't enough, as he reached out and shook Daddy's hand with a smile, Raveena saw the dimples.

Michelangelo couldn't have sculpted a better male.

At that moment the only thought running through her mind was:

How many love scenes were in the movie?

And . . .

Could they possibly add more?

Chapter 18

Siddharth nearly tripped as he got out of his car.

He managed to regain his balance in time and looked to see if anyone had noticed.

They hadn't.

Embarrassed, he arranged his features into a cool arrogant look—the one he'd perfected in many of his films—and started towards the group.

There was the annoying Randy Kapoor, Lollipop, with whom he'd worked in the past, and Veer. Veer was the best in the biz and a good man to boot. When he saw Daddy, his smile was natural and not forced like usual.

Although he only glanced quickly at the young woman, he took in everything about her from head to toe.

Siddharth was curious about what had brought his co-star all the way to Bombay. Many of his fellow actors and actresses in India dreamt of a Hollywood offer. Aishwariya, the highest paid actress in Bollywood, had two Hollywood offers on her plate. There was even talk she might be in the running to play one of the Bond girls in 007's next movie.

Siddharth stiffened as Randy patted his shoulder. "Sid, this is Raveena, your costar. Raveena, meet the biggest star in India."

Raveena smiled. "I'm looking forward to working with you."

Siddharth was a bit taken aback by Raveena's easy friendliness. Suddenly he was struck by a painful attack of shyness. He'd been affected by the problem since he was a kid. Because of his looks, he was often singled out. Women would come up to him on the street and pinch his cheeks and stroke his hair. Siddharth, a natural introvert, had dreaded these encounters.

As an adult, he still did.

Outside the studio gate, a crowd of female fans was openly goggling at him. Half of them looked as though their eyes would bulge out of their faces.

When he spoke, his words came out stiff and forced. "How are you enjoying Bombay, Raveena?"

"I'm still absorbing everything. Bombay is . . . so much."

Siddharth nodded at her response, and then quickly turned away. He wasn't good at polite conversation and preferred not to indulge in it.

Randy clapped his hands. "Come on everyone! I've ordered a lavish South Indian lunch."

Siddharth wanted to say something to Raveena, something witty and urbane, but he couldn't think of anything other than "How was your flight?" or "What's your favorite movie?" and those questions sounded dumb. So instead, he took a seat at the table inside next to Veer, and the two started up a conversation about location shoots.

Chapter 19

Isn't it nice when a gorgeous guy dismisses you with one casual glance?

Really does wonders for the self-esteem.

Of course, Raveena still wanted to jump on Siddharth and bite his neck, even if he didn't say one thing to her during the meal.

After a long lunch inside the air-conditioned studio spent gorging on South Indian cuisine—potato curry, coconut chutney, *dosas* stuffed with tomatoes, green chilies, coriander and onions and spicy lentil *sambar*—Randy had announced that the cast and crew were to report to the studio the next morning at nine a.m.

Raveena wasn't sure what exactly they would be doing the next day. Since there was no script, there wouldn't be the usual table read, and Randy had dismissed Veer's question about a storyboard.

She supposed she'd find out the next day.

While everyone jumped into their cars, Raveena hailed an auto-rickshaw to take her back to Uncle Heeru's.

* * *

Uncle Heeru wouldn't stop yelling.

The two plumbers he'd hired stood side by side and stared down at the ground.

"Cheaters! Duffers!" Uncle Heeru yelled.

Apparently, after the plumbers had shown up for work four hours late, Uncle Heeru had discovered them sprawled on the floor of the downstairs bathroom reading the newspaper instead of fixing the plumbing.

Eyes blazing, glasses hanging by one ear, Uncle Heeru turned to Raveena. "Does this happen in America? Indians have no work ethic! Bloody, lazy people!" He reached up, grabbed bunches of his hair and yelled. Then he turned and ran out of the room.

A few moments later he came running back—his arms filled with newspapers. He ran right past them and out the door.

Raveena moved to the window and watched as Uncle Heeru threw the papers to the ground and began stomping on them.

By the time her uncle returned inside, she informed him that the plumbers had left.

Uncle Heeru scowled. "Lazy useless duffers. I will watch them with an eagle eye tomorrow."

"You didn't fire them?" Raveena asked astounded.

He stared back at her puzzled. "I have removed the newspapers, now they have no choice but to work."

She guessed that was a solution of sorts.

Raveena spent the rest of the evening in her room reading *Hurray for Bollywood*—the book Maza had given her.

She was a quarter through the book when Nandini quietly entered to tell her she had a phone call.

Dressed in shorts and a tank top, Raveena followed her downstairs and to the hall extension. "Hello?"

"Raveena!"

"Mom!" she exclaimed happily. "What time is it there?"

"Ten in the morning. I thought your father would never leave for work. He's driving me crazy."

This was an all-too-familiar rant.

"So how are you? How is Heeru?" her mother questioned.

Raveena was tempted to say "hot" to the first question and "crazy" to the second. "We're both fine," she said instead.

Raveena then went on to inform her mother of the news of the day. "You'll never guess who my costar is on the film. I'm sure you've heard of him. Siddharth."

Her mother dropped the phone.

Raveena shouted her name a few times before her mother came back on the phone and asked in a breathless voice. "Siddharth? He's the number one actor in India."

"So I've heard."

"They worship him there. He's like a demigod. Such a beautiful man."

Thirteen thousand miles away, but Raveena swore she could feel her mother's sigh brushing against her cheek through the receiver.

"Well, I find him arrogant, Mom."

"You'd be too if you had crazy females chasing you down wherever you went," Leela snapped. "The poor boy can't even eat lunch in a restaurant. Women of all ages go mad for him. I read in *Filmfare* that while eating at China Garden with his family, the manager had to pull an eighty-year-old widow off of him. Poor boy can't eat in peace."

"That's no excuse for being arrogant," Raveena argued.

Her mother sniffed. "Hmmph!"

Raveena decided to get off the subject of Siddharth, since it was obviously a sensitive area. "Mom, can you call Jai and Maza and tell them I'm okay? Uncle Heeru doesn't have a computer, and I haven't been able to make it to an Internet Café."

Her mother agreed to do so, and they spoke of other things like family, friends and Bombay in general. Just as they were saying their good-byes, her mother brought up one last thing. "Do you know how much money Siddharth commands per picture?"

"No, Mom, but I'm dying to know."

This time Raveena *was* being sarcastic.

"Twenty crore rupees!"

"Crore? How much is that? I'm still figuring out the rupee-dollar conversion."

"Five million dollars!"

Okay, so it wasn't in the Brad Pitt or Tom Cruise range, but it was damn good for a Bollywood star. Siddharth probably lived like a maharajah.

Correction: a demi-god.

Meanwhile, the amount of money Raveena was getting paid rivaled that of the cast of *The Blair Witch Project*.

Her mother said good-bye, and Raveena walked over to the open window and leaned against the sill. She could smell jasmine and the sweet scent from the mango trees.

Once again, she needed to give herself a pep talk.

"Come on, Raveena," she said aloud. "We're talking Bolly-wood. If you can make it there, you can make it anywhere."

As far as pep talks go . . .

Raveena thought that was pretty damn good.

Chapter 20

The pain was so intense Raveena sat up in bed clutching her stomach.

Pushing her hair out of her face she glanced at the small digital watch on the nightstand.

Three a.m.

The intense heat of the afternoon had barely abated, but she was racked with chills.

Another sharp spasm of pain twisted her insides. She felt as though she'd swallowed a miraculously sharp set of Ginsu knives.

Shivering, Raveena got out of bed and turned on the light. Stumbling across the room, she opened the wardrobe and searched through her belongings until she found the bottle of Tums.

She shoved a few in her mouth, but her throat was so dry she could barely chew.

Without bothering with a robe, Raveena slipped out of her room, went down the stairs and headed towards the kitchen for a glass of water.

She was making her way through the darkened dining room when she tripped over something and fell to the floor.

She gasped when she saw what it was.

A human hand!

Raveena gasped twice more and the hand twitched.

Finally, her eyes adjusted to the dark and she could see what was in front of her.

Uncle Heeru was curled up under the dining table fast asleep.

Before Raveena could take in the scene completely, another wave of cramps gripped her stomach and bile filled her mouth.

She scrambled to her knees and ran to the nearest bathroom.

There wasn't time to wonder whether the plumbers had fixed the toilet or not.

Leaning over the seat she vomited for the next thirty minutes.

Since no one came to investigate, she assumed Uncle Heeru still snoozed underneath the table.

At that moment she couldn't care less.

Stomach finally empty, feeling about as frail as a skeleton with osteoporosis, Raveena curled up on the cool tile of the bathroom floor.

Then she came to two conclusions.

One, she had some sort of wicked food poisoning.

And two, she actually cared very much why her uncle preferred to snooze under furniture as opposed to on top of it.

* * *

"Amebic dysentery," the doctor said with finality.

Raveena looked up at him from under several layers of blankets.

"But," she protested. "I've been good. Nothing but filtered water. I haven't eaten anything off the street."

"What did you consume prior to disgorging?" the doctor asked.

"I had scrambled eggs here and *dosas* at the studio."

"Lavinia drinks too much Indian cola. Terrible stuff," Uncle Heeru said from where he hovered in the doorway. "She's killing herself."

The doctor ignored him. "No, it wasn't the cola. What was in the *dosa*?"

Raveena told him and added, "We all ate the same thing. I was about to call the director and see if anyone else is sick."

The doctor shook his head. "I doubt it is the *dosa*. Tell me about the condiments."

"Coconut chutney. And this jar of chili and vinegar."

"Ah," the doctor nodded. "How many chilies did you have?"

Just thinking about food made her want to hurl. "Well, I like spicy food. I had quite a bit."

The doctor fixed her with a stern look. "The chili juice was most likely made with contaminated water. A common problem."

"There was vinegar in it," Raveena objected. "Doesn't that kill germs?"

The doctor frowned. "Who told you that?"

"Nobody," she mumbled, feeling chastised.

The doctor wrote down a prescription for several items and turned towards Uncle Heeru. "Raveena needs to take—"

Uncle Heeru's expression suddenly became panicked. He threw up his hands and ran out of the room.

Annoyed, the doctor stared at Heeru's departing back, and then turned to Nandini who stood silently in the corner. "Take this to the chemist. Raveena must have two doses a day of each medicine for one week."

Nandini took the prescription and smiled. "Yes, doctor."

The doctor's annoyed expression relaxed, and he gently laid a hand on Nandini's head.

When he faced Raveena, his expression was once again stern. "Don't you know you can't eat everything in India? This is not America. You must be careful."

And on that note, he packed up his bag and took his leave.

Randy was perfectly fine with Raveena's not making an appearance at the studio.

"We have a group of journalists here who are interviewing Siddharth. It's fantastic publicity," he said.

"Will they want to speak to me as well? I'm pretty sick right now, but later—"

"No, no, there's no need for that," Randy assured. "They only want to talk to the *star*."

Raveena's dislike towards Siddharth grew stronger.

Raveena's dislike for Randy went without saying.

Raveena's dislike for food, at the moment, overwhelmed everything else.

"I have to vomit," she said.

The last thing Raveena heard before she flung away the phone and darted to the bathroom was Randy saying:

"Vomit? Are you ill?"

Chapter 21

The good thing about picking up an ameba or two is that you lose weight.

In Raveena's case, eight pounds.

It was seven days later, and she was ready to work.

Upon learning of her illness—Uncle Heeru phoned Leela to say Raveena was dying—her mother had called twice a day, and so had Auntie Kiran. Auntie Kiran had insisted Raveena send a stool sample via DHL so an American doctor could examine it. "Those Indian doctors are all quacks," she'd said firmly.

Needless to say, Raveena didn't listen to her aunt. The Indian doctor had spent almost an hour with her. The most she ever got out of her managed care physician back home was ten minutes.

Anyway, the proof was in the pudding, or in this case, the stool.

Raveena was ameba-free.

Nine a.m. sharp, Raveena had arrived at Sahara Studios after haggling with the auto-rickshaw driver over the fare.

Raveena was becoming quite adept at getting herself around, and she knew that it cost twelve rupees to go from her uncle's house to the studio. So when the driver demanded twenty, she argued like a local.

Granted, it was a matter of sixteen cents, but it was the principle of the thing.

Walking around, Raveena came to realize the studio was deserted, save for the old caretaker sweeping the drive.

Or, at least, it looked like the old man was sweeping.

Wielding a typical Indian hand broom made of twigs, he seemed to be sweeping the exact same bunch of fallen leaves back and forth. He wasn't making any progress.

However, Raveena wasn't about to lecture the man on his lack of a Puritan work ethic. Instead, she took a seat under the same coconut tree and waited for the rest of the crew to show up.

And waited.

Really, this waiting thing was getting old.

By ten the coolness of the morning had given way to wilting heat, and still no one had shown up.

The caretaker ambled towards her. "Why are you sitting here?" he asked.

"We're shooting today. I was told to be here by nine."

The old man smiled. He was missing several of his teeth. "No one will be here before eleven."

"But why did the director tell me nine?"

His smile widened. "Because that is the time to be here. Nonetheless, no one will arrive before eleven."

"Come," he beckoned.

Raveena followed him into the studio common area

where she'd overindulged in chilies and vinegar the week before.

He began flipping switches, turning on lights, and before long she heard the hum of the air-conditioner start up.

He disappeared for about ten minutes and returned with two steaming cups. "Chai," he said, setting one cup before Raveena with another of his gap-toothed smiles.

It was blistering and the air-conditioner hadn't fully kicked in yet.

Still, what else was there to do but drink hot chai?

Raveena raised her glass in toast and settled down for chai and conversation with the caretaker.

Maybe he could teach her a few choice Hindi swear words?

The ones her parents whispered, but she could never fully catch.

"Thrust! Thrust! Thrust!" Lollipop shouted above the music.

For Shiva's sake! Raveena was thrusting to the best of her ability.

Lollipop clapped his hands. "Cut!" The music was turned off.

Raveena was learning a lot on her first day at the studio. Violence in a Bollywood film is acceptable, but kissing isn't. Sex is taboo, but the suggestive hip rolls and pelvic thrusts she was performing in her dance routine were fine. Abrupt changes of location during songs are common—Scotland, Switzerland and New Zealand were favorite backdrops.

Randy had explained earlier to a disappointed Lollipop that he didn't have the budget for a foreign song shoot.

Panting, her hands on her hips, Raveena waited as Lollipop approached. It was hours later, and the rest of the crew had finally arrived. "The dance move is like this," Lollipop said and began to demonstrate.

He thrust out his hips, shimmied to the right, then left, executed a few classical Indian moves with his arms, and ended by looking over his shoulder, his eyes smoldering.

Raveena almost clapped. The man could move.

Since there still wasn't a script, Raveena spent the day rehearsing her first musical number.

In the song sequence, Mumtaz Mahal disguises herself as a provocative gypsy and sneaks into Shah Jahan's palace with her group of soldiers—also disguised as gypsies—and performs a seductive dance number in front of the Emperor and his men. The goal is to gain entrance into the palace so Mumtaz can murder Shah Jahan in his sleep.

Hence, Lollipop's smoldering look.

"You must be sexy," Lollipop instructed, lowering his eyelids demurely and slightly pursing his lips, "but at the same time the audience must see a hint of your contempt and anger towards the Emperor." Lollipop raised his eyes and flashed her with a burning gaze.

Honestly, Raveena was still trying to get her right hip to stay down while bouncing the left.

Nonetheless, she nodded. "Okay, got it."

The music started up again.

Getting the dance number down was important. Songs from Bollywood films were released prior to the film opening and their pre-release success was an indicator of potential box office returns.

Randy had hired the top music director in the country.

B. R. Hassan. Raveena heard Randy had to shell out a pretty penny for Hassan's services. No wonder she'd seen Daddy mopping his forehead more than usual.

But he was worth it. The soundtrack was sensational. Bass guitar, tabla and drums flowed together in something tribal, making her blood pound.

"From the top!" Lollipop shouted.

After spending the entire afternoon with the choreographer, Raveena had developed an immense respect for the man—and now managed not to giggle when she said his name or heard his high-pitched voice. After all, his job involved much more than choreography. He directed complex camera movements, set changes, costume design and anything and everything related to the musical numbers.

The fifty male background dancers behind Raveena began effortlessly mimicking Lollipop's instructions.

Raveena moved to the music, lip-synching to the singer's voice and trying to do the temptress-warrior thing when Siddharth entered the studio.

Staying in her line of vision, he leaned against the wall, folded his arms and watched.

The sight of Siddharth cool, composed and drop-dead delicious while she gyrated sweaty and flushed in her tank top and jeans—and still suffering the latent effects of dysentery—pushed Raveena's anger to the surface.

Glaring at him, Raveena whirled, spun, thrust, kicked and executed the Bollywood dance moves—mentally blessing her mother for forcing her into classical Indian dance lessons as a kid—and ended in the required pose, seething over her shoulder at the Emperor.

Lollipop bounced up and down. "Brilliant! Sexy and

filled with contempt!" He bounced over and wrapped her in a hug.

Raveena returned the bubbly choreographer's embrace. In the background, Siddharth raised an eyebrow, performed a mock bow in her direction and left the studio.

See.

All she'd needed was the right motivation.

Chapter 22

Raveena was attending her first Bollywood bash.

Randy Kapoor was throwing a huge party at his family's Juhu Beach estate. The crème de la crème of Bombay society would be there: stars, models, fashion designers, industrialists and socialites.

She had gotten her hair blown out earlier at the Rapunzel Salon—the one she passed by every day on her way to the studio. Unfortunately, just as she was led over to the basin for a wash, the power went out, and she sat in the dark while she was shampooed and conditioned with very cold water.

Raveena blessed the fact that she had not chosen a full body wax for the very same day.

Sitting in the dark, towels wrapped around their dripping hair, the patrons waited as various people fiddled with the generator struggling to start it. Finally, just as the generator sprang to life, the power came back on and the same people struggled to turn the generator off before it burned out.

Raveena's hair was then blown out by three dusky young

women—one to hold the dryer, another to hold the brush, and a third to divide the drying hair into sections. Well, there was an excess of labor in the country. Why use one person when you could use three? But the results were worth it, and she left the salon with a sleek mane of black silk.

Hair and makeup done, Raveena stood in front of the wardrobe wondering what to wear.

Uncle Heeru chose that moment to knock on the door and come in.

"Hi," she said over her shoulder, her arms filled with clothes.

Heeru walked over to the bedside table and picked up the copy of *Hurray for Bollywood*. "Is this book any good?" he asked.

"Yes. I'm almost finished if you'd like to read it." She dumped the pile of clothes on her bed.

Uncle Heeru frowned and set the book down. "This book will not help you while you are here. You must read the *Bhagavad Gita*. In it are all the lessons one needs to know about life. I have read it seven hundred times."

Raveena's mother had a beautifully bound copy of the *Bhagavad Gita* at home. The *Gita* was sort of like the Hindu Bible, a written volume of Lord Krishna's words detailing the nature of consciousness, the self, the universe and the ultimate path to self-realization.

One who truly understood and had studied the *Gita* would live a life of transcendence.

Earlier, Raveena had seen Uncle Heeru nearly run over the neighbors in his battered white Ambassador, then speed off without apologizing.

Hmm.

"I'll read it when I get home," Raveena said, picking out a black cocktail dress and shaking it out. It was a sweet little number by Marc Jacobs. She would need to iron it.

For some reason, Uncle Heeru was still hanging around her room, so she showed him the dress. "What do you think? It'll impress the Bombay bigwigs, right?"

Uncle Heeru looked aghast. "That dress is not appropriate! You will surely become the target of mischief-makers."

Raveena raised an eyebrow at the garment. It was sleeveless but was neither low-cut nor backless. She thought it was classy.

However, Uncle Heeru's eyes were bulging out in a way that was decidedly trout-like.

"Don't worry Uncle Heeru," she reassured. "I'll be wearing a light shawl over the dress." She didn't mention that the shawl was really a gauzy black length of chiffon.

Raveena was determined to look fabulous. She wanted to do LA proud. She had no intention of showing up at the party looking like the offspring of a hag and a country bumpkin.

It really had nothing to do with the fact that Siddharth would be there.

Really.

Uncle Heeru mumbled something and pulled at his hair. "I would like you to come with me to the temple on Tuesday. It will be a most auspicious day."

"Of course," Raveena answered. "I'd love to."

He nodded as if in agreement. "You will need Ganesh's blessings if you continue to remain in the film line. The industry is an ungodly place."

Raveena smiled politely and ushered him out of the room. "I really enjoyed our chat, Uncle Heeru."

Shutting the door, she returned to the wardrobe and prayed she hadn't forgotten her black lace Victoria's Secret bra.

Ungodly was the look she was going for.

"This is definitely a Page Three party."

Raveena turned to the young woman behind her in line at the bar. "Page Three?"

She had a short cap of dark hair and was dressed in low-slung cropped pants and a beaded turquoise bustier. Her belly button was pierced. "In Bombay, our Page Three is like New York's Page Six. If you want the latest in cocktail parties and glitterati gossip, that's what you read."

"Thanks," Raveena said and reached for her vodka tonic. Uncle Heeru subscribed to *Bombay Times*. She decided it was time to start reading Page Three.

Wandering around, Raveena didn't know what she'd expected from a party thrown by a Bollywood director. It seemed to be no different from an A-list Hollywood party. Not that she'd attended many of those.

The Kapoors' sprawling seaside villa, with a 180-degree view of the Arabian Sea, was enormous. A large Olympic-size pool complete with two waterfalls ran the entire length of the house. The decor was a mix of European tapestries, Mughal artwork and marble statues of Greek gods and goddesses.

Personally, Raveena thought it looked as though the Louvre had vomited up several of its collections.

Speaking of vomit . . . Randy appeared at Raveena's elbow and promptly offered to give her a tour of his bedroom.

Raveena promptly declined.

For a moment, Raveena thought she saw anger flash across Randy's eyes, but she was too distracted by his outfit to give it much thought.

Randy was wearing a black tank top, a black leather jacket—so much for the sacred cow—and black leather chaps with the crotch and seat cut out. Thankfully, he had on a tight pair of blue jeans underneath.

Well, truthfully, Raveena wasn't that thankful. His blue jeans were *very* tight.

To complete the outfit, Randy had hooked Bono-style sunglasses over the silver studded belt at his waist. His black hair had recently been highlighted with blond streaks.

Raveena was relieved to see Daddy, who greeted her warmly with his usual, "How are you, *beti*?" But then had to rush off when there was a crisis in the kitchen involving a platter of mushroom turnovers.

"I don't see Veer or Lollipop," Raveena said to Randy. She'd hoped to run into at least two people she knew.

"Celebrities only," Randy said. "Like me."

Raveena could see a suggestive leer forming around his lips and decided it was time to partake of some party food.

A trendy Bandra restaurant called the Olive Bar & Kitchen had done the catering, and the food was a blend of European and Asian cuisines. Raveena helped herself to vegetarian risotto and roasted pepper salad with feta cheese.

Spotting an empty chair, she sat down with her plate. The small group of women sitting around her were all in their twenties and early thirties. All were either beautiful, rich or both. And she couldn't help listening in on these glamorous creatures with their light, flirtatious, slightly exaggerated way of speaking.

She recognized the woman with flowing burgundy-tinted black hair and supermodel-like cheekbones sitting closest to her. Bani Sen. Currently the "it" girl in town, Bani had the distinction of being part of both the high society and the Bollywood scene.

As Raveena had learned, not everyone made the transition.

Bani had recently starred in one of Raveena's mother's favorite movies. Bani had played a sexy but virtuous woman who wins the heart of a serial playboy with her traditional values and high morals.

Next to Raveena, Bani laughed gaily and made several snide remarks about butt-fucking and blowjobs. She then demanded to know if anyone would share a line of coke.

Raveena wasn't a prude, but she had an image of her mother's face, happily watching Bani's movie, and she had to get out of there.

She was about to get up when Bani turned and smiled, her dark eyes cool and assessing. "So you're the one starring in Randy's new flick?"

Several of Bani's friends exchanged knowing glances.

Raveena didn't need to read the *Bhagavad Gita* seven hundred times to know what their looks meant.

They assumed she was sleeping with Randy.

She nearly spewed risotto.

"Yeah," Raveena said. "With *Siddharth*," she emphasized.

So she was bragging. She couldn't help it. These women were getting to her.

Bani's gaze turned mocking. "Oh, I know why Sid's doing it. He feels guilty. His father and Daddy were good friends . . . but what's your excuse? Shouldn't you be off in Hollywood making a film with Colin Farrell? I know that if I were from *LA*," she mimicked Raveena and emphasized the last word, "I would consider it a step down to come and work in India."

Raveena considered bitch-slapping Bani—surely that would put her on Page Three—but she respected Daddy too much and knew a WWF-type shakedown would surely cause the gentle man some embarrassment.

Instead, she smiled back at Bani. "You know, I never really thought of Bollywood as a step down." So she was lying. "But after meeting you, I really do feel like I'm slumming it."

And with that, she stood and walked away, her heart pounding.

She was close to tears. She wasn't a socialite or a glamorous creature, and she couldn't throw her head back, laugh gaily and discuss which was worse—an enema or anal sex.

Or at least not without a few drinks in her.

She went outside and stood at the railing, looking out at the sea. Moonlight glistened on the water. The gardens to her right beckoned, and she followed the small path leading away from the house, wanting to get far away from the party.

It was there in the center of a gazebo dripping with star jasmine blossoms that she ran into Siddharth.

He was sitting on a white marble bench with his head in his hands.

At the sight of her he grimaced. "Shit. You didn't follow me, did you?"

Raveena burst into tears.

Chapter 23

Siddharth wondered if the rumors were true.

Was Raveena sleeping with Randy Kapoor?

Well, that would explain the crying.

She sat down next to him on the marble bench and wiped ineffectually at the tears with the back of her hand.

Siddharth reached into the pocket of his slacks and pulled out a handkerchief. Silently, he handed it to her.

"Thanks," Raveena muttered and dabbed at her face. "I know why I left the party, but why did you?

What was he going to tell her? That India's answer to Brad Pitt felt uncomfortable in a room full of people?

His aloofness was in actuality a painful shyness. And that shyness was especially evident around members of the opposite sex. They expected him to be a stud like in the movies, a consummate lover.

Immediately after his first brush with success, Siddharth had been set up with the niece of a family friend. His recent success had given him some newfound confidence. After dinner, while walking the girl to her door, Siddharth had prepared to take his leave when the girl threw her arms around his neck and pressed her lips to his. "Oh, Siddharth," she moaned.

Siddharth had had a good time that night and decided to kiss the girl back. After a moment, she pulled back and stared up at him with disbelief. "You're a horrible kisser," she'd exclaimed. "What are you, a virgin or something?"

Flushing red, he'd turned around and ran to the lift, the girl's mocking laughter following him.

He'd noticed the way the female guests stared at him, their gazes full of expectation. The men in the room shot him looks laced with jealousy. Siddharth felt like a fraud. That was why he'd left the party.

"I needed some fresh air," he told Raveena.

"I'm feeling homesick," she said quietly. "God, what am I—six?"

"It can't be easy," he said. "Away from your family and friends. Thrown into the masala moviemaking."

"Masala?"

He smiled. "Another word for mainstream Indian filmmaking."

"Oh." She laughed. "I like that."

Siddharth liked her laugh. For some reason, it made the tension in him ease away.

"How do you like working on this film?" Raveena asked.

Siddharth shrugged. "It's the same kind of role I'm used to. I'm tired of being typecast."

Raveena snorted.

Siddharth turned to her in surprise.

"Sorry," she said, "but you don't know the first thing about being typecast. You're the biggest actor in India. This is the first leading role I've ever been offered in my entire career, and it's not even in the same hemisphere."

"I have my pick of roles?" Siddharth said, outraged. "The audience, the producers, the directors only want me to play the same character over and over again. The strong romantic hero. I want to play drug dealers and mafia dons or maybe even a transsexual who dresses in saris and sings at weddings."

"So what's stopping you?"

Siddharth hesitated. He wasn't used to spilling his secrets, but Raveena seemed truly interested, not just pretending. "I played a man who seduces young women and then forces them into prostitution," Siddharth smiled in remembrance. "It was wonderful fun."

"What happened?"

He was suddenly bitter. "The movie failed miserably. It was a total bomb."

Raveena crossed her legs and adjusted her dress. Siddharth was distracted by the smooth curve of her thigh. There was something very sexy about that dress, the way it seemed so conservative but then revealed a sudden flash of creamy skin. He gazed at Raveena thoughtfully.

"Big deal," she said. "So the movie bombed."

"So? So people in Bihar actually began rioting and threatened to burn down the theater. They didn't spend their hard-earned money to see me play a villain."

"What I mean is . . . didn't you ever have one of your so-called formulaic films flop?"

He thought about it. "Yes, two or three actually."

"Well, see!"

"See what?" he demanded.

"Maybe your villainous film just sucked? Maybe it had nothing to do with your performance." she said. "But that was one film! Even Tom Hanks doesn't have a super hit with each and every film."

Raveena had a point, Siddharth thought. He'd enjoyed Tom Hanks's film *The Terminal*, but it hadn't struck a chord with audiences, and it had been directed by Steven Spielberg! "Now, this is what my manager Javed should be telling me," he said aloud.

Raveena laughed. "You know," she mused. "I can't remember what I was crying about before."

"Sid! What are you doing out here?"

Bani Sen stood before them.

"Oh, right," Raveena murmured. "Now I remember."

Chapter 24

Raveena wondered if anyone had ever thought of constructing a BOLLYWOOD sign amid the parched hills above Bombay.

Then again, what with the heat haze, exhaust fumes, sea mists and monsoon showers, the sign would most likely be barely visible.

Anyway, Raveena didn't need a sign to remind her she was in Bollywood.

The fact that there was a Moroccan dance number in the middle of a film about the Taj Mahal . . . that was sign enough.

Raveena was lifted up by a team of male dancers and placed before Siddharth in the makeshift tent.

The dance didn't seem to advance the plot at all. All Lollipop had said was, "It's a slave dance, very come-hither, seductive and sexy. You've been captured by Siddharth and are his slave. But he will become a slave to your heart."

Got it.

Randy had spent the previous winter in Marrakech and wanted to incorporate the look into his film.

Raveena was sort of proud of herself for learning the dance moves in one solid hour.

She swayed before Siddharth, her veils flying as she spun, and prayed the material wouldn't snag on her teeth.

She hadn't seen Siddharth after their conversation at Randy's party. He'd been quiet on the set as well, staying in his trailer and watching movies.

Raveena felt he could have at least invited her in to join him.

She didn't have a trailer.

She did have an air-conditioned dressing room, though, and had spent most of her time there finishing *Hurray for Bollywood*.

But now, as Siddharth placed his hands around her waist and pulled her against his chest, she could swear the intense way he gazed at her wasn't just acting.

Or was it?

And what was up with him and that Bani bitch?

"Cut!" Lollipop shouted.

The music stopped, and Siddharth dropped Raveena as if she had an infectious skin disorder.

"I've got it!" Randy shouted, running into the studio and waving a stack of bound paper.

They all turned to face him.

Looks like Randy has finally finished the script, Raveena thought.

"I just finished the first five scenes." Randy said happily.

Several of the people in the studio began clapping.

Raveena glanced at Siddharth, but he had a bored look on his face.

Oh well, she shrugged.

It was time to start memorizing lines.

And then she realized something.

Mumtaz Mahal, the seventeenth-century Mughal Empress of India, was going to have an American accent.

Raveena decided to go to the Karma Productions office and approach Daddy instead of Randy with her request.

It wasn't a hard call. Daddy never ogled her breasts or pinched her ass and ran away giggling.

"It's essential for suspension of disbelief that my Hindi be flawless," she pointed out after she'd taken a seat. "The audience needs to feel like they're in seventeenth-century India."

"Excuse me, sir," Millie said, entering the office. "But the set designer is on the phone and would like to know when she should begin production on the Eiffel Tower replica."

Raveena cocked an eyebrow. "Eiffel Tower?"

Millie smiled. "Oh yes, ma'am, for the eight wonders of the world song sequence. The designer has done a wonderful job. Wait until you see."

The Eiffel Tower was built in 1889. Mumtaz Mahal and Shah Jahan had met in 1607.

Raveena uncocked her eyebrow.

So much for suspension of disbelief.

"Thank you, Millie," Daddy said. He reached for the telephone and smiled at Raveena. "I think a dialect coach is an excellent idea. I know just the one."

Exiting Karma Productions, Raveena sucked in her breath as the air-conditioned coolness was replaced with intense heat.

She sucked in her breath again when she was nearly sideswiped by a familiar green BMW.

Randy lowered his window and winked at her. "Raveena, baby, can I give you a lift?"

She opened her mouth to say no when the cool, recycled air inside the car bathed her face. Auto-rickshaws filled with sweaty passengers zoomed up and down the road.

On one hand, she'd have a cool ride but one shared with Randy and his cologne-doused body. On the other, she'd be Randy-free but sucking exhaust in the back of a rickshaw.

She made eye contact with the AK-47-wielding guard in front of the building, but he didn't help her with making a decision.

"Screw it," she muttered and jumped in Randy's car.

"So what were you doing here?" Randy asked. "Looking for me?" He pursed his lips suggestively. "How about dinner tonight? I'll drop you, go home, have a shower and change."

Raveena had an image of Randy in his black leather chaps minus the jeans and gagged. She cleared her throat. "Actually, I came to see Daddy about hiring a dialect coach. He agreed."

Randy's expression became sulky. "Daddy's not the director. I am. You should have approached me. I would have said yes."

The next few minutes were decidedly sulk-filled.

"So," Randy pouted. "Will you have dinner with me tonight? There's no shooting tomorrow."

Raveena had another decision to make. She longed to say no. Still, she was working hard to make her role a success. It didn't seem smart to hire a dialect coach to help her perfect her acting ability and then annoy the director.

"Dinner sounds like fun," she spit out.

"Tonight?"

"Tomorrow would be better." She needed twenty-four hours to mentally prepare herself.

"Tomorrow night then," Randy agreed. "It's a date."

Raveena stared out the window as Randy turned up the volume and began rocking out to the Turkish techno beat.

She gave him a sideways glance. His arms were soft and flabby.

Tomorrow night with Randy, if worse came to worse . . .

She could easily take him.

Chapter 25

The next day was Tuesday, and Raveena spent the morning with the dialect coach.

Mrs. Mirza lived in a brightly decorated one-bedroom flat with her husband. Both her children were grown and settled in America.

Mrs. Mirza had a doctorate in Hindi and had been a lecturer at St. Xavier's College before she retired. "We will work on accent reduction and modification," she said in her light lilting voice.

After a morning spent with the jolly, gray-haired woman, Raveena learned how tongue placement and the usage of different mouth muscles could make her indistinguishable from a native Hindi speaker.

She couldn't wait to try her accent out on her parents. They usually laughed at her when she tried to say certain Hindi words. Raveena thought their behavior rude, which only caused them to laugh more.

As a result of their excellent session, Raveena was back at Uncle Heeru's for lunch.

Her uncle was pleased to see her, and for a moment she couldn't understand why.

And then it dawned on her.

It was Tuesday.

Temple time.

Uncle Heeru took Raveena to Siddhivinayak.

The 250-year-old temple was devoted to Lord Ganesh and located in central Bombay.

It was also the first Hindu temple to go online.

Uncle Heeru explained that followers from across the globe regularly made donations to the temple via the Web site.

Apparently, all you had to do was Google Ganesh.

Uncle Heeru went to Siddhivinayak every Tuesday.

And as they pulled up in his old white Ambassador, Raveena realized that a majority of Bombayites did too.

Tuesday was the most auspicious day of the week and the crowds rivaled those of Disneyland on a summer afternoon.

Uncle Heeru had already crossed the busy street and was heading into the thicket of devotees without looking back to see where Raveena was.

Praying to Lord Ganesh she wouldn't become road kill, Raveena took a deep breath and darted across the traffic-clogged thoroughfare.

Barefoot, Uncle Heeru was waving at her from the side of the temple. "Lavinia!" he shouted.

"You must remove your shoes here," he said as she joined him.

"Here?" Aghast, she looked down at her favorite pair of Cole Haan slides.

She knew she'd have to remove her shoes but she hadn't expected the hordes of suspicious-looking worshippers.

Raveena spied a man who was taking shoes and giving people a ticket in return. She ran over to him and handed over her shoes, the required ten rupees and took the dirty paper slip with a number on it.

He then let loose a stream of betel juice from the corner of his mouth, and half of it splashed on her bare feet.

"What are you doing?" Uncle Heeru demanded. "This man is not to be trusted."

"Well, I can't just leave my shoes by the side of the road. Won't they be stolen?"

"Most probably," Heeru said philosophically. "Come now."

Having been well-trained by her mother, Raveena had brought a scarf and now wrapped that over her hair and joined the snake-like queue of people waiting to get into the temple.

As they neared the door she noticed they didn't have any offerings.

She poked Uncle Heeru in the back. "We can't go inside empty-handed. I'll go and buy some flowers." An old woman was selling marigolds near the entrance.

Uncle Heeru reached into his jeans pocket and pulled out two Almond Joy bars and handed one to her. "This will make the God happy. He loves coconut." He cast a disdainful look at the flower-seller. "What will he do with wilted blossoms?"

Holding the candy bar and whispering a prayer of apology to Lord Ganesh if it was melted, Raveena shuffled her feet and entered the temple.

The smell of sandalwood inside the darkened interior was intense.

The combination of smoke and heat made her head spin as she was jostled and pushed forward by the crowd.

"You will only get thirty seconds in front of the God," Uncle Heeru said.

"What?"

Maybe it was due to the close proximity of their Lord, or the heady scent of sandalwood, but the worshippers behind Raveena began to shove with abandon.

People began to chant.

Jai Ganesh! Deva!

Before she realized it, Raveena found herself mumbling. *"Jai Ganesh. Jai Ganesh."*

The air grew thick, and as the smoke parted she realized Uncle Heeru was no longer in front of her.

The crowd, overcome with divine love and passion, surged forward, and Raveena was nearly knocked to the floor.

She grabbed hold of the railing, looked up and found herself directly in front of an immense black marble statue of Ganesh.

It was magnificent.

The people behind were pushing for their turn to stand in the line of God, and she quickly put the Almond Joy at the feet of the statue and closed her eyes in prayer. An immense feeling of serenity washed over her. She prayed for her family and friends. And since Ganesh was the remover of obstacles, Raveena prayed her time in Bollywood would turn out for the best.

Well, she did have a career to think of.

The next moment the woman behind her shoved and she was forced to move forward.

Outside, she took a breath of fresh air and her head immediately cleared.

Raveena returned to the shoe guy and retrieved her slides—intact and safe.

She then bought a bottle of water to wash her feet before sliding them back into her shoes.

It was almost three, she was ravenous, and Uncle Heeru was nowhere to be found.

However, his ancient white Ambassador was still parked by the side of the road.

Her growling stomach couldn't wait, so she headed for the nearest snack stand.

Raveena bought a large paper plate of Bombay *chaat*. A spicy mix of rice krispies smothered in potatoes, tamarind and mint chutney, yogurt and various masalas.

It was heaven.

And she wasn't just saying that because she stood near a temple.

Ever since her illness, Raveena had been able to eat anything and everything without a hint of indigestion. It was like she'd developed a gut of iron.

She wolfed her snack down and looked for a trashcan.

There were none, of course. She'd yet to see a single trashcan in the entire country.

People were throwing their empty plates onto the street.

Raveena nudged the little girl who'd just thrown her can of coke into the gutter. "You know the best thing about India?"

The little girl looked at her curiously.

Raveena smiled. "You can toss the trash on the floor."

The girl walked away.

"I'm kidding!" Raveena called after her.

She took her empty plate back to the vendor. "Please dispose of this. I don't believe in littering."

The man took her plate and then chucked it into the bushes behind him.

Whatever.

Turning around, Raveena finally spotted her uncle.

He was weaving drunkenly through the crowd.

"Uncle Heeru!" She ran towards him.

His white hair was sticking up in all different directions, his glasses were hanging precariously on the end of his nose, and his shirt was stained and partially unbuttoned.

"What happened?" she asked.

He smiled sluggishly. "Do you know how to drive?"

Raveena looked out at the traffic-clogged road. Buses careening wildly, taxis weaving in and out ignoring stoplights, and street kids and beggars darting between the cars.

Raveena turned back to Heeru who was tilting from side to side.

Damn!

Chapter 26

By *the grace of Ganesh, Raveena hoped to make it safely back to* the house.

As it turned out, Uncle Heeru had mistakenly drunk what he thought was ordinary buttermilk, but really was buttermilk spiked with an opiate.

Not as uncommon as it sounds.

The drink, *bhang*, is commonly sold in many religious spots throughout India.

The alternate reality produced by *bhang* is thought to bring one closer to god.

So as Raveena negotiated Bombay traffic, her hands clenching the wheel in a death grip, Uncle Heeru deliriously described the sexual encounter he'd just had with the Goddess Lakshmi.

"Why don't you try and sleep, Uncle Heeru?" Raveena said, as she shifted clunking gears.

"Very good, Lavinia," Heeru mumbled, closing his eyes.

Luckily for Raveena, the city of Bombay was basically composed of one main road. All she needed to do was keep going straight until she hit Turner—the large petrol station on the corner would serve as her landmark—and then make a left. Unfortunately there was only one lane going each way and the traffic was horrendous.

Raveena had a sudden longing for LA gridlock.

She focused on just going straight, driving at a snail's pace, and trying not to get sucked up into the melee of taxis, motorbikes, buses and, yes, once again, the odd cow.

At every junction, demigods of the Indian screen gazed down on her from enormous billboards. The muscle-heavy actor Salman Khan brandished a machine gun in the ad for his new movie. The star of *Bride and Prejudice*, Aishwariya, pouted behind designer shades.

Shah Rukh Khan, the charismatic cutie, displayed his Omega watch, and Amitabh Bachchan raised a gracious toast on behalf of Pepsi.

Stuck at a light, Raveena stared up at the billboard of Amitabh Bachchan. He was her mother's all-time favorite Indian actor. The Big B, as he was affectionately known, was so popular in India, he was considered a living legend. He'd been starring in movies since the 1970s, playing cops, criminals and everything in between, wearing white slacks and wielding a gun in one hand while fighting off a sultry temptress with the other.

According to the stack of gossip-heavy glossies Raveena had purchased, Amitabh Bachchan had reinvented himself, swapping his heroic past for patriarchal roles and hosting the Indian version of *Who Wants To Be A Millionaire?*

And then there was Siddharth . . . leveling a killer gaze in the ad for his new film, *Love in Sri Lanka*.

The dimples weren't out, but his face was still killer.

Sweat dripping down her face, Raveena hit the clutch and braked behind a massive truck with the words "keep distance" sprayed on the back.

Oh yeah, she had every intention of keeping her distance.

They stopped along what looked like a block of office buildings. Raveena glanced casually to her left to check on Uncle Heeru when she saw two young men openly peeing against the side of a building.

Even worse was when Uncle Heeru saw them. She thought he'd been sleeping. Instead, he rolled down his window, started shaking his fist and screamed, "*Junglees! Cleanliness is next to godliness!*"

The two men turned, nudged one another, grinning, and began to saunter towards the car. One of them had not bothered with zipping up his trousers.

"Uncle Heeru," Raveena warned.

"That is a public building!" Heeru shouted. "These poorer classes have no respect. *Junglees*, all of them."

Raveena didn't think the young men, poor or not, appreciated being called wild animals.

Thankfully, the traffic started up, and she put the car in gear before the men could reach them.

They continued to inch along, and Uncle Heeru was now wide awake. "Indians have ruined this country!" he shouted to no one in particular.

Raveena tried to ignore him.

She was unsuccessful.

Uncle Heeru was on a rant.

"Did you know I was once arrested by the government? The bastards thought I was a spy for Pakistan!"

Raveena didn't know whether it was the *bhang* talking, or if Uncle Heeru was serious.

Since they were once again at a standstill, she had no choice but to listen.

"As your mother may have told you, I am considered a very spiritual man," Heeru began. "When I was fifty-two, I decided to fulfill a lifelong dream of bathing in the mouth of the Ganga River."

"Ganga?" Raveena asked.

"You know, the Ganges," Heeru said impatiently. "The Ganga begins high up in the Himalayas. It is there the water is the purest and holds mystical qualities."

"Like what?"

"Mystical qualities," Heeru repeated. "I hired a guide in the town of Gangotri. I did not trust him, but he was the least loutish of the bunch."

The world, according to Uncle Heeru, seemed to be filled with louts and *junglees*.

"Together we began the journey towards the mouth," he continued. "Along the way we came across a swami meditating on a rock. My duffer of a guide had gotten us lost, and I assumed that the swami, being such a wise man, would know where the river began. So I politely tapped him on the shoulder."

At that moment traffic moved forward again, and the car ahead was blasting *bhangra* music so loud it was impossible to hold a conversation.

A motorcyclist pulled up next to the Ambassador, and the driver raised his arm and rested it against the hood. This meant his armpit was directly in Raveena's face.

She nearly fainted from the smell.

Angry, she knocked the stranger's arm away, and as they pulled forward, Uncle Heeru resumed his story. "What I did not realize," he narrated, "was this wise man had reached the last day of his seven-day meditation, and my polite tapping had awoken him early. He stood up and began pelting me furiously with rocks."

"Some swami," Raveena said.

"No, no, he had just been about to reach enlightenment when I disturbed him. Naturally, he was quite angry. Somehow, as we ran away, we found ourselves back on the correct path. And soon, I was at the holiest of holy spots, the mouth of the Ganga."

Raveena nearly cried with relief—not because her uncle had made it to his holiest of holy places—but because she saw the petrol station that marked her turn. Very carefully, she made the left.

Heeru, unaware of Raveena's emotional state, continued with the story. "So, I insisted the guide avert his eyes, and I removed all my clothing in preparation for immersion in the sacred water. Filled with heavenly abundance, I danced into the icy coldness, dunked my head in the blessed waters, and when I surfaced, it was to see the ruffian of a guide running off with my clothes and my new Nike runners from America."

Finally, they were on Portugal Road and moments from home. Raveena couldn't wait to fill the bathtub with some blessed waters.

Heeru went on. "It was with great relief that I spotted a pair of military police in their jeep. Unfortunately, my lips were frozen with cold, and I had difficulty managing sentences. The policemen deduced that I had been trying to swim across the border and arrested me on the spot as a Pakistani secret agent."

"How did you get free?" Raveena asked as she turned the car into the drive that led up to the bungalow.

When Uncle Heeru didn't answer she looked over to see him sleeping.

Shaking her head, Raveena stopped the car, opened all the doors so her uncle would have some sort of a breeze, and entered the house, leaving Heeru to his nap.

Chapter 27

Raveena was still in a spiritual mood after her sojourn to the temple.

So she prayed for a miracle to keep Randy from arriving for their date.

Like a horde of rampaging elephants causing a traffic jam?

Unfortunately, Randy was on time.

Indian standard time, that is.

He was forty-five minutes late.

By the incessant honking of his horn, Raveena deduced Randy wasn't coming in to get her.

Uncle Heeru stood in the doorway peering suspiciously out at the night. "What is that noise?"

Raveena thought the least Randy could do was get out of the car and say hello to her uncle.

Then again, Uncle Heeru would most likely deem Randy the worst type of mischief-maker.

"I won't be late," Raveena said. Not if she had anything to say about it.

She crossed the courtyard and opened the car door.

Randy was wearing a black leather beret, a white cotton tunic and turquoise velvet pants. He grinned. "Hey, baby."

Somewhere between entering the restaurant and sitting down, Raveena decided that she hated Randy Kapoor.

Really and truly hated him.

Randy reached for the plate of shantung prawns and served Raveena a small amount while generously adding the rest to his plate. "I prefer working with first-time actresses. They have more at stake and are easier to convince into doing . . . things." He winked.

Raveena aimed a sharp kick to his shin.

"Ouch!"

She blinked innocently. "I'm sorry. Bad leg cramps. Calcium deficiency, you know."

They were at China Garden, the most popular Chinese eatery in Bombay.

Ordinarily, Raveena would have enjoyed herself tremendously. The food was fantastic. *The New York Times* had proclaimed China Garden one of the best restaurants in Asia.

If only Randy hadn't hogged all the crispy Golden Dragon duck.

Randy reached for her hand and began playfully tracing her palm with one of his sticky, stubby fingers, leaving a trail of plum sauce across her skin. "I love American women. They don't have all the hang-ups Indian women do. American women will have sex on the first date." Randy giggled.

Raveena poked Randy's arm with her fork.

"Stop that!"

"Sorry," she said with even more innocence. "Arm cramp. I really need to drink more milk."

Randy gazed at her suspiciously.

The maître d' walked past their table and caused Raveena to look up. She stiffened as she saw Siddharth and Bani being seated.

Great, they probably thought she and Randy were on a date.

Bani caught Raveena's eye and smirked. Leaning over the table she whispered something to Siddharth. He turned and gazed at Raveena. His expression was blank.

Randy jumped up and practically ran to their table. "Sid! Bani!" he exclaimed.

Raveena longed to bury her face in the mound of spicy Shanghai noodles.

Then she heard Randy say her name and something about dating, and she shot out of her chair.

"Ah, here's your girlfriend, Randy," Bani said with a cool look. "Nina, right?"

Why were people in India having such trouble with her name? "Raveena," she corrected. "And I'm not Randy's girlfriend."

"That's right. Raveena and I are dating. It's our first date," he said suggestively. "These American women move fast."

Raveena was so angry she could hear a peculiar rushing in her ears. But her career was more important than what that bitch Bani thought. The fact that Siddharth just sat staring at his plate instead of acknowledging her presence only exacerbated her anger.

"Randy," she said with false sweetness. "Can we please leave?"

Randy nudged Siddharth. "See what I mean?"

Back in the car, Raveena decided she may as well fish for

136

information. "I didn't know Bani and Siddharth were such good friends."

"Siddharth's a lucky man. Bani is sexy as hell and filthy rich. Her father is Bengali Sen, the steel tycoon. Both families are keen on a match between the kids."

"They're engaged?" Raveena asked with disbelief. She didn't think Siddharth and Bani looked like a couple, but then that was Bollywood for you.

Seeing is disbelieving.

"Not yet, but everyone expects to hear an announcement soon. I don't want to talk about them," Randy said with a touch of crankiness. "I want to talk about us. There's a lovely secluded spot on the Bandstand. Why don't I park the car and—"

Raveena recalled the *Lonely Planet*'s description of the Bandstand becoming a veritable lover's paradise after dark.

She needed to think up an excuse fast and one that would not hurt Randy's feelings. A happy director proved for a happy working environment.

Raveena would have to use every shred of tact in her being to field Randy's nauseating advances.

"Before we hit the Bandstand, do you mind stopping at a shop? I need to pick up some sanitary napkins—my flow is extra heavy tonight."

Randy slammed on the brakes. "Your flow? Maybe I should just drop you home. You probably want to be alone at a time like this."

Men and menstrual cycles.

The two did not mix.

"Oh, no," Raveena said cheerfully. "I'm having a fabulous time. Do you think you could run in and pick up the pads for me? Oh, and some Vagitsu tampons as well? I seem to be out of cash. And please ask the clerk if they carry any feminine rinses." She added a line straight from Uncle Heeru. "Cleanliness is next to godliness."

Without another word, Randy drove her straight home and sped off before she was fully out the door.

Swinging her purse, Raveena sauntered through the front door.

Hadn't she told her uncle she'd be home early?

Chapter 28

The next few weeks began to take on a weird sort of regularity, even if masala filmmaking was anything but regular.

Raveena would email her family and friends from the Internet Café every morning and then head to the studio around eleven.

Back in America, her father had bought some new three-piece gabardine suits, her mother had won the last kitty at her card game, Jai was mulling over switching from MAC cosmetics to Urban Decay, and Maza had dumped her gynecologist and was deep into her second novel, titled *If These Vaginal Walls Could Talk*. And there was good news from Brussels. Rahul and Brigitta were engaged. Brigitta had gone from girlfriend to Flemish fiancée.

Raveena had also begun reading Page Three every morning while drinking her Nescafe coffee. As it turned out, she wasn't the only American actress in town working on a Bollywood film. Bo Derek was there with her bikini along with two former *Baywatch* babes.

Raveena was the only one whose name wasn't in print, though.

However, she was putting in numerous hours swiveling her hips, enacting bizarre situations, exaggerating her emoting and fulfilling every other basic requirement of a Bollywood box office bonanza.

Dialogue turned out to be remarkably easy—even if she was handed her lines while in makeup—because it seemed all of her dialogue in the movie put together totaled two sheets.

Meanwhile, in one week of shooting, Raveena had fifty-seven costume changes and wore sixteen different wigs.

The last wig gave her a rash.

But what really itched was Siddharth's aloofness.

And after she'd given him such brilliant career advice!

On screen, Siddharth, the idol of the silver screen, seduced the industry and the women of India in a flurry of triceps and biceps, tight T-shirts, and slick dance moves. But as soon as the cameras stopped, Siddharth closed up emotionally and retreated to his trailer.

Raveena decided she may as well return to her dressing room. On set, Randy was demanding a big chase scene with Siddharth behind the wheel of a Ferrari. Veer reminded him that the story was supposed to take place during the 1600s.

Raveena was just getting out of her chair when the studio doors opened and a gaggle of schoolgirls in Sacred Heart school uniforms spilled into the studio.

"Where's Siddharth?" they demanded in unison.

"This is a closed set," Randy said angrily and was nearly trampled by the girls as they rushed towards him like a school of fish.

"He's in his trailer," one of the girls said, and the shrieking mass of fans filed out.

One girl was left behind—the one who'd known where Siddharth was. Her black hair was tied in two braids and her small face was dominated by a thick black unibrow. Her hazel eyes were beautiful, though, clear and wide. In fact, something about the young girl's gaze struck Raveena as very familiar.

The girl saw her staring and managed a tentative smile.

Raveena instantly smiled back. She hated to make a generalization—okay, she didn't really mind—but she found the women in India rather distant and cool. It wasn't unfriendliness. Raveena was just used to people back home in the States being more approachable.

Besides, she hadn't made a single friend since she'd been in Bombay and was lonely for company. "Hi, I'm Raveena."

"I know," the girl said. "My brother told me about you."

"Brother?"

"Siddharth. He doesn't usually talk about his costars, but he's mentioned you a few times. I'm Sachi."

Raveena forced herself not to grab Sachi and demand to know verbatim what Siddharth had said about her. Instead, she tucked her hair behind her ear and affected an air of indifference. "He talks about me? How interesting."

Sachi's gaze was amused. "It's fine if you're in love with my brother. All the girls in my school are mad about him."

Quickly, Raveena changed the topic. "So, were those your friends you came in with?"

"Some of them are. The rest . . ." Sachi furrowed her brows in an expression that was rather ferocious. Raveena

141

almost stepped back. "The rest are just using me to get to my brother. Girls are so stupid!" she said angrily.

Raveena felt a pang of sympathy for Sachi. "Listen, I was about to go for a Thums Up. Join me?"

Sachi looked at her with surprise. "You like that drink? It tastes like cough medicine to me. Anyway, I have to go home. Mummy's sending the driver to pick me up from the studio."

Raveena shrugged. "Okay, maybe next time."

"Wait," Sachi said. "Would you like to come with me? Have dinner with us?"

"I'd love to."

Honestly, Raveena's motives were pure. She already liked Sachi. And she was tired of dinners spent conversing with Uncle Heeru.

And really, truly, her answer had nothing to do with the off chance she might run into Siddharth at home, enjoying a shower.

A hot, steamy shower . . .

Chapter 29

Siddharth's mother, Poonam, reached for Raveena's plate. "Have some more rice pilaf, darling."

Even Raveena, with her new rock-hard bowels, couldn't take another helping of food. She held up her hand. "I'm ready to burst."

"Very well," Poonam said. "But darling, you're much too thin. How do you expect to carry children without extra padding?"

Raveena had never in her life been called thin. She wasn't overweight, but the closest she had ever come to thin was the term "healthy."

But Siddharth's mother thought she was thin.

Even though the woman was a food-forcer, Raveena quickly found herself liking her.

Raveena had been slightly disappointed to discover Siddharth wouldn't be joining them for dinner. She had wanted to ask his family where he was, where he was going and whether he really was dating Bani Sen, but she thought that might look a bit tacky.

Nevertheless, she was glad to have met Sachi. The girl was a spitfire.

"Mummy," Sachi fumed, "why do you talk to every single woman about children? Why don't you ask them about their careers or their dreams or even what their favorite color is? You're inhibiting my emotional growth. Bloody hell, it's the twenty-first century!"

Poonam wagged a finger. "Your brother would never talk to me like that."

"That's because you don't bother him with talk of marriage and children," Sachi argued.

"Actually, darling, I do. I nag him about it incessantly."

"Oh, right," Sachi said glumly.

Poonam sat back as the family servant, Juggu, entered to clear away the dishes. "Thank you, Juggu," she said and lit up a cigarette with a fancy gold Zippo.

Raveena was surprised by Siddharth and Sachi's mother. In Bollywood films, widows were always portrayed as subdued, white sari-wearing women whose only purpose in life was to see to their children's happiness.

Poonam's social calendar was full, she was very attractive, wore makeup, cut her hair short and wore a beautifully cut *salwaar kameez* that highlighted her trim figure.

When Raveena had commented on the lovely outfit, Poonam had patted Raveena's cheek and said, "Thank you, darling, it's a Ritu."

Raveena's Page Three reading was coming in handy. She knew Ritu Kumar was one of the top designers in India and regularly designed the outfits for India's entry into the Miss Universe pageant.

"Sachi, I can't stand it," Poonam said, tapping her cigarette into the ashtray. "Please, darling, thread those eyebrows of yours."

Sachi folded her arms across her thin chest. "Why? So I can become a sexual object like Siddharth? No thank you, Mummy."

Mother and daughter continued to argue.

Meanwhile, Raveena realized the numerous Thums Ups she'd consumed at the studio were catching up with her.

"May I use your restroom?" she asked and then wondered if she should have waited for a gap in conversation before asking.

"Of course," Sachi said. "But you'll have to go upstairs. The downstairs loo isn't working." She pushed back her chair. "I'll show you."

"Finish your dinner," Raveena said. "I'll find it."

"Darling, it's up the stairs and the first door on your right. Directly across from Siddharth's bedroom," Poonam added.

Hmm.

After washing her hands, Raveena really had every intention of going back downstairs.

Well, maybe she'd only take a quick peck at Siddharth's room.

She was only human.

In fact, she'd be considered rather odd if she were *totally* devoid of curiosity.

Ten minutes later Raveena was taking a casual peek into Siddharth's closet to see if he favored the preppy or club look when his bedroom door swung wide open.

Damn.

Caught in the act.

How clichéd could you get?

Chapter 30

"*What are you doing?*" Sachi asked.

Raveena let out a deep breath. Thank God it was Sachi and not her brother. Still, the situation was a tad awkward. "I'm, ah, snooping through your brother's things." she admitted.

Sachi walked into the room. "Well, then, let me show you where he keeps the good stuff."

Forty-five minutes later, Sachi and Raveena were sitting on Siddharth's bed flipping through his photo albums after going through his drawers.

Raveena did feel a bit guilty about the drawer thing, but it had been Sachi's idea after all.

"What's going on here?" Siddharth demanded, standing in the doorway.

"Oh, hey, Sid," Sachi said. "We're just going through your stuff."

"What's this?" Raveena held up a heavy bronze statue.

"That's his CineStar Award," Sachi answered. "He won it for best actor. Stupid, huh?"

Raveena disagreed. "I don't think so."

"In a way, Sachi's right." Siddharth took the statue from Raveena. "The award shows are all rigged. It's not like the Oscars."

"Well," Raveena said with a small smile, "Some people say the Oscars are all politics. If you play it right . . ."

"Darlings, where are you?" Poonam flowed into the room. "Siddharth, your dinner is getting cold."

"Ma, I told you I ate dinner out."

"Darling, you're too thin," Poonam protested. "All of you are too thin."

Raveena was suddenly nervous she'd get stuck eating dinner again as well. "Actually, I think I'd better get going. Uncle Heeru will be worrying."

Truth be told, when she'd called her uncle from the studio to tell him she wouldn't be home for dinner, it had taken him a few minutes to remember who she was.

"This is Lavinia," she'd said finally.

"Lavinia isn't home," Uncle Heeru said and hung up the phone.

"I'll give Raveena a lift," Siddharth said quickly, practically grabbing Raveena's arm and propelling her towards the door.

"Wonderful, darling," Poonam called out. "It's too late for her to be taking an auto."

"Bye," Sachi leaned against the banister and waved.

"Bye," Raveena waved back. "Come by the studio again, okay?"

"I will," Sachi answered. "If I can get past all of Sid's girlfriends."

"Brat," Siddharth muttered.

They exited the front door, and Siddharth punched the

button for the lift. "Listen," he said, running his fingers through his hair. "I could use a drink. How about you?"

Uncle Heeru didn't approve of alcohol, and Raveena hadn't had a drink in ages. Her liver was happy, but she wasn't.

"You read my mind," Raveena said.

Chapter 31

Siddharth drove to Zenzi.

The sumptuous, glass-paneled, wood-floor lounge struck just the right chilled-out ambiance. Since it was the middle of the week, the room was populated but not crowded.

The manager nearly jumped when he saw Siddharth and immediately led them to a discreet table in a dark corner. He then insisted the first round would be on the house—a vodka martini for Raveena and a Scotch, neat, for Siddharth.

The music was low, soothing, a funky mix of western, Indian and Arabic notes, and Raveena recognized the beats of Buddha Bar. She had all six Buddha Bar CDs.

For a moment, surrounded by the décor and designer labels, sipping her expensive cocktail, Raveena felt as though she were in London or Tokyo, rather than a mile or two from some of the planet's largest and most squalid slums.

But that thought was sort of a downer.

"Sachi invited me over for dinner," Raveena explained, just in case Siddharth thought she had found out his address by stalking him.

"I knew Sachi would like you. I told her you were easy to talk to."

Easy to talk to? She and Siddharth had hardly exchanged more than a few words.

Then again, according to Griffin, Raveena did a lot of emoting with her eyes.

"Sachi's great," Raveena said. "She may just be my first friend in Bollywood." Although she and Nandini had sort of a bond. Nandini was teaching her Marathi—a local dialect—and Raveena was teaching her English.

There was a long gap of silence.

"Siddharth," Raveena said suddenly, "what do you think of this film we're doing? I don't mean to be negative, but what was up with the scene we filmed today? The script doesn't fully explain why Mumtaz hates Shah Jahan so much."

Siddharth finished his drink and signaled the waiter for another round. "You have to understand. We need to appeal to a mass audience. These movies are pure entertainment. It's an evening of escapism for poverty-stricken people, and the uneducated are not going to walk out of the theater asking, 'Now what did the filmmaker mean by that?'"

"I think you and Randy Kapoor are underestimating the Indian audience," Raveena said. "I was reading in *Screen* that out of every 250 films released in Bollywood, only one is a super-hit and five are hits. The producers of most of these movies are spending millions on shooting scenes in Switzerland and trying to cram in as many shots of the Alps as they can, but the audience—poor, rich, whatever—doesn't buy it."

Siddharth sighed and shook his head. "I don't know . . .

in my heart I try to stay hopeful. The Indian film industry is so important. What with all the communal violence in India . . . Muslim against Hindu, Hindu against Sikh and Brahmin versus untouchable . . . well, just look at the cast and crew of our film. Veer, our cinematographer is Sikh, I'm Hindu, and you're—"

"Half Hindu, half Sikh."

"Right, and the music composer, Hassan, is Muslim, Audrey D'Cunha, the makeup artist, is Catholic, and Lollipop . . ."

"What is Lollipop?" Raveena asked, curious.

Siddharth scratched his head. "I, ah, don't know. But my point is that Bollywood is a unifier. And by the way, I hate the word 'Bollywood.' The Indian film industry is unique and complex, not some Hollywood offshoot. The South Indian film industry based in Madras—"

"Ah, Tollywood," Raveena said with a smile. The regional language of Madras was Tamil. Tamil plus Hollywood . . . well one got the idea.

Siddharth looked as though he was going to argue, and then shook his head and smiled.

Damn those dimples, Raveena thought.

"I wish my mom could meet you," she said.

A look of pure panic passed across Siddharth's face.

Shit! "No, wait, I don't mean . . . it's not that I want to marry you or anything . . ."

Siddharth was now looking very afraid.

God damn it!

What was wrong with her? She'd only had two drinks, and she was by no means a lightweight. She took a deep breath. "When I was a kid, and I'm talking like four or five years old, my most vivid memories are of my mom and I curling up on the couch with a bowl of popcorn and settling down for a three-hour Indian film. Inevitably, I'd fall asleep before the end, and my dad would come downstairs, pick me up and carry me back upstairs to my bed. We watched *Sholay, Qurbaani, Laawaris . . .*"

Raveena carefully watched Siddharth's face and was relieved to see him relax.

"Your mom is a fan?" he asked.

"She's seen every one of your films."

Siddharth cocked his head and smiled.

Raveena felt her stomach clench, and it wasn't from the rice pilaf.

Relax, she told herself. So you haven't been on a date since the Clinton era. Get a grip.

Determined to not freak Siddharth out again by looking lovelorn, Raveena babbled on. "There was even this movie theater in downtown LA that used to show Bollywood movies. I would dress up in my pajamas, my mom would put pillows and blankets in the back of the station wagon and we would drive into LA with her friends and their kids. On the way home all the kids would curl up in the back and sleep."

Siddharth opened his mouth to say something when the waiter sidled up. "Sir? Ma'am? Another drink?"

Siddharth looked down at his watch. Raveena noticed it was a Rolex. "We'd better go," he said.

Raveena would have liked to stay the whole night, but that didn't seem like something to say out loud. Siddharth paid the bill, and within minutes, his Mercedes had pulled up in front of Uncle Heeru's house.

"Thank you for the drinks and the ride," she said. She placed her hand on the door handle and waited, but it didn't look like Siddharth was going to grab her and press his lips on hers.

Finally, he turned to her, his hazel eyes looking almost black in the darkness. Raveena caught her breath. "Is the door handle stuck?" he asked. He reached across her and opened the door.

"Thanks," Raveena said flatly.

As soon as she was safely inside, Siddharth sped off, the smooth motor of his car soundless in the night.

Chapter 32

Days turned into weeks.

Siddharth continued to ignore her on the set except for the polite nod here and there.

Raveena continued to email her family and friends every morning from the Internet Café.

She and Sachi also began hanging out at least once a week, trying out different coffeehouses and restaurants. Their favorite place unanimously was the Dosa Diner in Bandra.

Raveena also got used to dialogue changes being scribbled on napkins moments before the camera rolled.

And Raveena refused to wear the wig that kept causing her to break out in a rash. It didn't make sense anyway, how in one scene her hair was down to her butt and in the next she was sporting a curly perm—especially when both scenes supposedly took place on the same day.

Raveena was also not invited to any more Page Three parties. That's what happened when the current "it" girl, Bani Sen, turned out to be your arch-nemesis.

Wasn't that dramatic?

Raveena also began spending her off hours going to the movies with Nandini and Nanda.

And she finally began to get the Bollywood formula.

First of all, people burst into song in all kinds of unlikely places. The movie they saw on Monday featured the hero, chained up in a dungeon, breaking into song and executing a few dance moves with his shackled feet.

Secondly, while Raveena would begin rolling her eyes at the whopper of a plot—like the one where the bullet-ridden, unconscious son spurs to life when his mother's honor is insulted and soundly thrashes the offender—the audience would burst into tears. Nandini and Nanda held each other and sobbed.

Third, Masala style basically meant a film that combined comedy, drama, romance and music together.

There were also a few key differences between a movie theater in India and one in America. American theaters didn't carry masala-flavored Ruffles. American theaters didn't have Nescafe coffee machines in the lobby. In American theaters your soda came in a plastic cup with ice.

Then again, one didn't really want to order ice in an Indian movie theater because it was probably made from tainted water, and besides, all sodas were served in glass bottles, which you had to guzzle in the lobby before you returned to your seat.

American theaters did not have audience members whistling and stomping their feet every time a musical number came on. Nor did they have male audience members shouting at the heroine to "Shake it, baby!"

Lastly, American theaters did not have a special section

for "ladies" where women could sit and not be bothered by the whistling, foot-stomping males.

When her movie came out, would the males in the audience whistle and shout, telling Raveena to "shake her rump!"?

Most probably.

Still, by spending all her off hours with Nandini and Nanda, she was able to learn a few things about Uncle Heeru. Like why he was so odd.

After seeing the latest Bollywood offering with the girls—a story that revolved around a beautiful village girl who enjoyed bathing under waterfalls and a handsome city boy whose parents forbade him to ever consort with village girls—Raveena returned home with the girls and learned that her uncle had been jilted at the altar by the love of his life.

"She was a Chinese woman," Nandini whispered as she shelled peas for dinner.

Nanda, who was peeling potatoes, nodded in agreement.

"What happened?" Raveena asked.

"Your uncle joined his brother Jagdish in Hong Kong. Together they opened a jewelry store. One day this Chinese woman came into the store to buy some diamond earrings and that was it. Love at first sight."

Raveena was in shock. One of Uncle Heeru's favorite rants was against caste mixing. One should only marry someone from the same caste. And here he had fallen in love with someone not only from a different class, but a different culture.

Nanda picked up the rest of the tale. "Heeru and the Chinese woman began seeing each other in secret. But Jagdish found out and informed the other brothers and sisters. They were all dead-set against the match. But Heeru ignored his family and proposed to the woman with a ring he had designed himself. She agreed and a date was set. Heeru arrived at the church—"

Raveena interrupted, "A church?"

"Yes," Nandini said. "The woman was Christian."

Raveena had also heard her uncle rant against interfaith unions. Hindus should only marry Hindus and so forth. But he had fallen in love with a Christian.

Nanda threw the last peeled potato into a bowl and wiped her hands. "When Heeru arrived at the church, it was empty. He waited and waited, but neither the bride, nor her family, came. You see, the Chinese woman's family was just as opposed to the marriage as Heeru's. Only, she did not have the strength to disobey them in the end."

"That is so sad," Raveena said.

For the first time, Nanda smiled at Raveena and lightly touched her hand.

"Yes, it was very sad," Nandini agreed. "Heeru left Hong Kong and returned to Bombay to take care of his aged mother. When she died she left the bungalow to him."

Raveena suddenly empathized with her uncle's bizarre behavior. However, his tragic romance did not fully explain why he continued to snooze under tables and inside the TV cabinet.

Maybe there was a story there as well?

Chapter 33

Raveena stopped insisting on a bound script and plot coherency from Randy.

It was like talking to a brick wall.

An extremely thick brick wall.

Especially when everyone else, even Siddharth, seemed content not to rock the boat.

Speaking of the boat scene . . .

Mumtaz—the warrior princess—escapes from Shah Jahan's men and commandeers a boat to take her back home. She is halfway down the river when Emperor Shah Jahan leaps out from behind a mast and surprises her.

Mumtaz immediately pulls a scimitar she had somehow hidden inside a skirt that barely grazes her crotch and lunges at the emperor.

The two scuffle from the bow to the aft of the boat until Mumtaz finds herself positioned under Shah Jahan's body. She struggles wildly, but he subdues her by pinning her arms above her head.

Mumtaz spits in his face, which apparently turns the emperor on, and his lips loom closer and closer until it looks as though the two are in for some tongue-twisting.

And then a storm breaks out.

Together the two ride out the horrendous weather conditions until the next morning when daylight breaks and the water is once again still.

It is then they realize that the boat has drifted far upriver and they are lost.

Meanwhile, along the banks of the river, happy villagers celebrate the harvest with song and dance.

This is when the emperor and the warrior-princess begin to fall in love.

Needless to say, the boat scene was not filmed on a real river. A boat was constructed inside the studio, and Randy used jump cuts to go from the studio boat to footage Veer had previously shot of a river miles away in the countryside.

Raveena looked at the dailies and was aghast.

This was the film that was supposed to propel her to stardom?

This was the film that was supposed to do for her what *Devdas* had done for Bollywood actress Aishwariya?

Damn it! Raveena wanted to be in the running for the next Bond girl!

Or at least in the running for *Kama Sutra 2* if director Mira Nair chose to make a sequel.

Veer gave Raveena a sympathetic pat on the shoulder and went out for a cigarette.

After everyone had left, and the kind, gap-toothed

caretaker had begun to turn off the lights, Raveena sat in the dark with her face in her hands.

She had the sinking feeling that in the entire history of Bollywood films that had bombed . . . *Taj Mahal 3000: Unleashed* was going to break all the records.

Chapter 34

Siddharth wandered through the empty studio, running his hands along the freshly constructed sets.

This had been one of his favorite things to do in the early days. Experiencing firsthand what it took to create that movie magic.

Soon, laborers led by the set designer would begin construction on the Emperor's palace, created from wood, papier mâché and paint.

When Siddharth had asked the set designer why his team didn't make use of CGI (computer-generated imagery), the designer explained that the low-cost manpower in India—the daily rate for a carpenter is a couple hundred rupees (four dollars)—made the cost of hiring a few hundred to build sets cheaper than anything high-tech.

Siddharth ran his hand along the fake prow of the boat and tried to re-create the old movie magic thrill.

Nothing.

And he almost walked right by Raveena without seeing her.

She was sitting in the dark, her chin resting on her hand. Although he couldn't see her expression, he knew she was down.

Why else would she be sitting alone on an empty set in the dark?

"What are you doing here?" he asked.

"Feeling sorry for myself," she mumbled without looking up.

"What happened?"

"I saw the dailies."

Siddharth let the breath escape between his teeth. "I would have advised against that."

"This is going to be a horrible film," Raveena said angrily. "I've been watching a lot of Indian movies and most of them are a cut above Randy's. In fact, I was pretty damn impressed with a few. I would love to work with those directors. Hell, I'd rather have starred in Randy's remake of *Runaway Bride*."

Siddharth winced. "Don't say that."

Raveena was once again silent.

Siddharth wanted to make her feel better. He felt guilty about his aloofness towards her, but every time he thought of starting up a conversation he'd hear that girl's jeering voice in his head. "And *you're* the heartthrob of India?"

But then he remembered how she'd counseled him in his hour of need. "Listen," he said, "Daddy has hired one of the best editors in town. And you never know; this film might strike a chord with the audience. Show business is a shot in the dark."

Raveena looked up hopefully. "The best editor in town?"

"Yes," Siddharth lied. Truth be told, he'd never heard of the editor Randy would be working with. But he wasn't lying about moviemaking being a gamble. He'd seen some of the worst films resonate with the audience and become super hits.

"You're right," Raveena said, the heaviness gone from her voice. "What do I know about how Bollywood works? This could be the greatest film ever!"

Siddharth wouldn't go that far.

"I went too far, didn't I?" Raveena asked.

They walked outside. It was almost eight in the evening, and Bombay residents were out in full force. The work day was over and shops were full; the relative coolness brought families out to hit the food stalls.

God, Siddharth loved this city.

Suddenly, he wanted Raveena to feel the same way. To-morrow was a Muslim holiday, Eid.

"Have you seen much of Bombay?" he asked.

Raveena gave him a rueful smile. "I'm embarrassed to say I haven't. But I'm getting to know the neighborhood of Bandra pretty well."

"How about a tour?" he suggested. "Tomorrow?"

"Definitely."

"Pick you up around eleven?"

"Perfect."

He hailed an auto-rickshaw for her and waited until she got in.

And then he hopped into his Mercedes.

He was having dinner with Bani tonight at Spices, the Asian-themed restaurant at the Marriott in Juhu Beach.

At one time he'd enjoyed Bani's company, but now he found himself getting together with her because he felt obligated, because their families were friendly, and because with Bani, it was always easier to say yes instead of no.

Chapter 35

That night Raveena sat down with Uncle Heeru to watch the number one soap opera in India:

Maa Ka Pyaar
A Mother's Love

She had read in Page Three that the creator of the soap, Esha Sharma, had a business degree from the University of Michigan and an MBA from Harvard. Both Esha's parents had been Bollywood stars in their heyday, and their Ivy League-educated daughter had tripled the family fortune by starting a production company that produced the top five soaps in the country.

Uncle Heeru was glued to the TV from nine to nine-thirty every Wednesday.

On the television screen, a widowed mother in a white sari dragged her injured son up the steep steps of a temple and single-handedly threw his body down in front of the statue of Lord Krishna.

The mother beat her chest and sobbed. She berated the god, screamed, sobbed some more, and then demanded that Lord Krishna heal her son. As if to further the point, the mother grabbed her son's head and banged it against the altar several times.

The mother was crying, Uncle Heeru was crying, and suddenly the statue of Lord Krishna began crying.

Raveena had to hand it to Esha; she had tapped into the Indian psyche. No doubt her old professors at Harvard would be proud.

When the phone rang and Uncle Heeru made no move to answer it, glued as he was to the storyline, Raveena went into the hall and answered.

"Chica! How are you?"

"Maza!" Raveena yelled.

"Silence is golden!" Uncle Heeru shouted from the sitting room.

Raveena dropped her voice several notches. This wasn't the eighties, when Raveena's mother would have to scream into the receiver just so Raveena's grandparents could hear her. "I can't believe it's you," Raveena said happily. "What's going on? How are you?"

"Spill it, chica," Maza said. "I want to hear about Siddharth. Emails just weren't doing it for me."

Raveena sat down in the chair by the phone stand and curled the cord around her fingers. "Maza, I feel like such an idiot. I've fallen for a Bollywood hunk. I'm sure it's all lust."

"And what's wrong with that?"

Raveena could hear her friend taking a drag on her cigarette. "I don't know . . . it seems so 'high school' to be falling for a movie star."

"You're an actress, chica—who else are you going to meet? I say bang him."

"It takes two to bang. I don't think the guy is into me. He did invite me to go sightseeing tomorrow, though."

"Sweetie, why would the guy waste his day with you if he wasn't interested?" Jai asked, cutting in.

"Jai?" Raveena laughed. "How are you? Where are you guys? What time is it there?"

"Eleven, honey, and we're at Maza's. I'm trying to coax her into a makeover. She refuses to wear anything but eyeliner."

Raveena smiled, feeling better than she had in weeks. "God, I miss you guys."

Maza was back on the line. "How's Bollywood treating you?"

"Well . . . it's chaotic, haphazard, undisciplined, the director is sort of a prick, and I don't think anyone in the industry even knows that I'm in town."

"So it's like you're doing an independent film," Maza said. "Except for the director being a prick—that's more big-budget, right?"

Trust Maza to put it in perspective.

Raveena laughed again. It felt good to laugh. "You hit it on the head, chica. Now, tell me how you and Jai are doing and then hang up. I don't want you getting stuck with a big-ass phone bill."

"Big deal, that's what money is for. Anyway, Jai decided not to leave MAC, I'm way behind on my deadline, as usual, and I've decided to swear off men."

"Maza! You can't. You know I live vicariously through you."

"Well, now I'm going to do it through you. Make me proud. It's about time you found a guy of your own. And he's beautiful."

"How do you know what he looks like?" Raveena asked.

"I looked him up on the Internet. How can a man that stunning even function? He doesn't have any issues, does he? The good-looking ones usually do."

Raveena thought about Siddharth and his moments of friendliness followed by aloofness. "Umm . . ."

"Never mind, sweetie," Jai was back on the line, "help him work through those issues. You know I always advised you not to date Indian guys because of their mama-complex, but Siddharth is too luscious to pass up. You deserve him."

Her friends rang off soon after, and Raveena decided to call it a night. It was only ten, but she needed to choose her outfit for tomorrow and get her beauty sleep.

Peeking into the sitting room, she saw Uncle Heeru curled up under the coffee table.

Chapter 36

It had been a sleepless night.

Raveena was plagued by dreams of Siddharth and her alone in a bed surrounded by filmy mosquito netting in the middle of the jungle. Siddharth was dressed in tight leather pants and was shirtless but wore a necklace of tiger teeth.

Even her dreams were turning into cheesy Bollywood movies.

She was also plagued by a baby fruit bat that flew in through her open window and screeched furiously as it struggled to find a way out.

Raveena leapt out of bed, unsure of whether to run away or attempt to help the bat, when, screeching, it flew up and got tangled in her long loose hair.

Her screams woke Nanda and Nandini, and they came running. Together the girls were able to remove the bat from Raveena's hair and safely set it free outside.

This time when Raveena thanked them, Nanda gave her another small smile.

Uncle Heeru was meditating in front of the picture of Sai Baba and was not to be disturbed.

Raveena thought that if all tour guides looked like Siddharth, India's tourism would triple.

He started the tour at the Gateway of India, the most popular landmark in the city.

According to Siddharth, in the days when most visitors came to India by ship and Bombay was the principal port, the sandy monolith of an arch had served as a beacon to India. The monument had been open to visitors since 1924.

Directly across from the Gateway was the plush and majestic Taj Mahal Palace & Tower Hotel, situated on the waterfront, and overlooking the harbor.

Siddharth left his car with the valet at the Taj Hotel. "Let's head over to the Gateway."

They had taken only a few steps before he was mobbed.

Men, women, children, rich, poor, young, elderly, surrounded them. They didn't want an autograph; they wanted to touch the movie star. Some just gazed, wide-eyed, while others pulled on his shirt and grabbed his arms.

Since it was a holiday, the crowds were out in full force. Raveena thought about throwing herself in front of him as a human shield but ended up grabbing his hand and running with him to the safety of the hotel lobby.

"Wow," she said teasingly, "you really are a demigod."

"Would I sound like a spoiled bastard if I said I hate that kind of shit?" he asked.

Raveena looked back outside to where some of his fans still lingered, desperately trying to peer into the hotel. The imposing Sikh guards at the entrance, though, kept them away.

"No, you're not a bastard," she said. "I think celebrities do occasionally have to sign autographs and pose for pictures—it's only fair to the fans—but what happened outside . . . that was way over the top."

He gazed at her thoughtfully. "I know where you can get a nice view of the gateway and the harbor."

They strolled through the lobby. "I would love to stay here," Raveena mused. She had never seen such a beautiful hotel lobby. The Moorish influence was everywhere, blending wonderfully with contemporary Indian touches—vaulted ceilings, onyx columns, silk carpets and crystal chandeliers.

The Harbor Bar seemed filled with tourists and wealthy Bombayites, but of course Siddharth was able to get the best table with a spectacular view of the Arabian Sea.

The martini list was extensive, and the bar also featured a selection of excellent cigars. Since it was almost one p.m., and she didn't know if she'd get another chance to spend the whole day with Siddharth, Raveena thought to hell with it and ordered a dirty martini. Siddharth settled for a beer brewed in India—called Taj Mahal, natch.

There were a few interested glances cast their way, but thankfully they were left alone.

Siddharth leaned close and whispered, "See the tall man puffing on a cigar behind me?" Raveena stole a quick look and nodded. "That's the Maharajah of Lalpur."

Raveena stole another look. She noticed the Maharajah's long hands, high cheekbones and heavy-lidded eyes. The massive ruby on his finger was magnificent. "He's single," Siddharth added.

She raised an eyebrow. "Is he . . . ?"

"He's not gay. He's lazy. In an interview he said he doesn't have the energy to sustain a relationship."

The Maharajah caught Raveena staring and gave her a slow, sexy smile. Next to him, Siddharth looked like a boy.

Raveena shook her head. She was turning into as big a snob as Uncle Heeru. The Maharajah was probably a royal asshole.

"The Maharajah turned a majority of his land into a wildlife preserve. He's on the committee to save the Bengal Tiger from extinction," Siddharth said, offering up some more details.

"What are you? His matchmaker?" Raveena said crossly. She didn't like her narrow-minded judgment of royalty being questioned.

Siddharth grinned and his dimples made her forget all about the Maharajah of Lalpur.

Siddharth asked her if she was hungry—she wasn't—so they got back in the car and headed for a magnificent section of Victorian architecture Siddharth explained was known as *Kala Ghoda* or "black horse." The area was named after a bronze statue of King Edward VII astride his dark horse that had once graced the premises.

The area was now a parking lot.

They drove past the University, the National Gallery of Modern Art, the Prince of Wales Museum and the Jehangir Art Gallery.

Siddharth then drove past an area called Flora Fountain and pointed out the Bombay Stock Exchange.

They passed by the VT, the beautiful Victoria Terminus railway station that looked more like a Gothic cathedral than a place to disembark.

Opposite VT was the Victorian *Times of India* building, which housed Bombay's daily newspaper. Raveena wondered who the Page Three staff would write about next.

Siddharth was an excellent tour guide. He knew the history of the city like a scholar, and his words were full of pride as he pointed out his favorite locations.

Raveena reflected that after eight years in LA, she could probably take a visitor to the Farmer's Market and the Getty Museum. That was about it.

"This stretch of road is known as the Queen's Necklace," Siddharth said, as they drove along the coast. "At night, when all the streetlights are on, if you look down on Marine Drive all you see are a row of lights against the darkness of the water, and it looks like a necklace."

He pointed to the tall buildings on his left. "The flats here are worth millions in American dollars."

Meanwhile, street kids ran up and down the drive selling flowers, cheap copies of books and, of course, Bollywood magazines.

Raveena realized that India was not a third-world country. It was two worlds—a first world and a third, both existing simultaneously.

"Ma'am, *Harry Potter* . . . *Harry Potter*, ma'am."

Outside Raveena's window, a little boy waved copies of J.K. Rowling's famous series.

"Please, ma'am, *Harry Potter*?" The boy had a wistful look on his face.

Raveena already had the first five books in the series in hardcover. Nevertheless, she bought the faded copy of *The Order of the Phoenix*.

"Thank you, ma'am!" The boy flashed a bright smile.

"Here," Raveena said, handing the book to Siddharth. "Have you read any of them?"

"No."

"Now you can start."

"Do you want to buy me the rest of the series?"

Puzzled, she didn't get what he meant until their car was besieged by at least a dozen kids all waving copies and shouting, "*Harry Potter*, ma'am! *Harry Potter!*"

"Uh oh," Raveena said.

Laughing, Siddharth indicated the kids. "You're dealing with some of the best business minds on the planet."

The day passed like a whirlwind for Raveena. There was so much to take in.

She bought several gorgeous Fendi knockoffs at the Oberoi shopping arcade in Nariman Point for her mother, Maza and herself.

They had a seafood lunch of fresh crabs cooked in a green garlic curry and a Bombay specialty fish called pomfret, which was cooked tandoori style.

In the evening they went to Bade Miya, a food stall that was open from dusk to one A.M. and served the best kebabs in the city. The kebabs came in rolls and were served with a spicy sauce, lime, and no napkins.

Siddharth had come prepared, though, and he supplied a box of tissues as they sat in the car and ate.

"Look at this guy," Siddharth said with amusement.

Raveena turned and laughed at the sight of a large stray dog, his paws on the window sill, his face peering in through the open window.

"Here," Raveena said and passed along her last kebab, which Siddharth handed to the dog.

Siddharth then put two fingers in his mouth and whistled. The man who'd taken their order hustled over to the car. Raveena admired people who could whistle like that.

In fact, she found it downright sexy.

And it was the smart thing to do, as other people were vainly trying to catch the man's attention by waving and yelling.

Siddharth ordered a plate of kebabs for the hungry dog.

Raveena found that even sexier.

Chapter 37

Too soon it was dark out, and they were heading back to Uncle
Heeru's.

Raveena didn't want the day to end. She couldn't invite
Siddharth up to her place because she didn't have a place.
What would her uncle think? What would Siddharth think
of Uncle Heeru?

Besides, the vibes Siddharth was giving her were friendly
but hardly sexual.

She didn't even catch him glancing at her boobs, for
god's sake!

Raveena had never, ever made the first move with a guy.
But now she wondered . . .

There was a first time for everything.

"You know, I've never been to the Bandra Bandstand at
night," Raveena said, in what she hoped was a casual voice.

Great, now she was taking cues from Randy the letch.

"We can drive alongside it," Siddharth replied, "it's on
the way to your uncle's place anyway."

Not exactly the response she was going for.

Thinking furiously, as they seemed to zoom by the Bandstand far too quickly, Raveena cried out, "Ooh! Stop here! Look at the view!"

Siddharth stopped the car.

The area around them was too dark to see anything. They could barely make out the water from the seawall.

"Isn't it beautiful?" Raveena gasped.

"You can't see anything," Siddharth pointed out. "Maybe if we head back to the lighted—"

"No!" Raveena shouted. Siddharth stared at her in surprise. "I mean," she said gently, "someone might see you, and the next thing you know we'll have a horde of fans surrounding the car. Let's just . . . sit here for a while."

They sat in silence.

And sat.

Raveena needed to try harder. Obviously the ambiance wasn't cutting it. She reached for his hand and in a flirtatious voice said, "I never noticed your watch before. Is it a Rolex?" She let her fingers run lightly against the inside of his wrist.

Siddharth looked down at his watch. "No, it's a Tag. I do have a Rolex, though. I collect watches." He pressed the side of the watch and the dial lit up. "We should be heading back."

It was now or never.

"Siddharth," she said.

He turned to her.

She put a hand on either side of his face and kissed him.

He didn't pull away, but he didn't exactly kiss her back either.

Still kissing him, she sat up on her knees, wrapped her arms around him and put every ounce of passion into her kiss.

One of her knees hit the lever against Siddharth's seat and the entire seat went back, along with Siddharth and Raveena on top of him.

She pulled away and stared down into his face. What had she done? The Bombay heat was obviously making her crazy! "I'm so sorry," she said. "Maybe I have a brain disease. I didn't mean—"

Siddharth reached up and pulled her back down against him and kissed her.

Yes! Raveena thought.

Siddharth pulled away. "I can't do this."

No!

"I understand," she whispered and began to slide over to her seat.

"Where are you going?" he said and pulled her back. He flipped them around so she was under him and he was on top, his arms against her sides, supporting his weight. "Your elbow was digging into my spleen," he explained. "This is much better, no?"

"Much," she murmured.

Siddharth began to kiss her softly, on her mouth, along her face, her neck . . .

Time ceased to exist.

Well, technically, since the dial on Siddharth's watch was still lit up, she knew exactly how much time had gone by.

Still . . .

She wanted him to take her right then and there. Wanted to feel his hands on her breasts, her vulva . . .

Vulva?

Before Raveena could wonder where that thought had come from—

There was a loud tap against the window and a light shone in their eyes. Siddharth lifted his head and Raveena pushed back her mane of hair.

"Shit!" Siddharth cursed.

Two policemen stood outside the car.

In a flash, Raveena was back in her seat and Siddharth opened his window.

"This is not allowed," the policeman said sternly. "Residents have complained about couples parking their cars and engaging in dirty acts."

Siddharth and the officer began arguing in Hindi. The second officer, silent, was shooting Raveena leering looks.

Then with an angry thump of the wheel, Siddharth started the car.

"Are they letting us go?" she asked.

"No. We have to follow them to the station."

"But," Raveena protested, "don't they know who you are?"

"That's exactly why we have to go with them," Siddharth answered tightly. "Usually they're looking for a bribe, but thanks to the new police commissioner, they intend to make an example of me."

Raveena felt awful. "I'm so sorry, Siddharth."

He didn't answer.

Chapter 38

Life seemed to go downhill after that.

Siddharth paid the 1200 rupee fine—40 bucks—and they were allowed to leave.

Naturally, the head officer on duty had called a reporter from the *Times*, and Siddharth and Raveena were photographed exiting the station.

Their ride home was silent.

The next morning, sipping her Nescafe, Raveena saw she had finally made Page Three.

Mega-watt star Siddharth arrested for lewd public behavior with American-born B-movie actress Raveena Rai . . .

B-movie actress?

Well, it was several letters up from her normal D-list status.

She'd tried all morning to call Siddharth, but no one picked up at his flat, not even Juggu.

She'd even tried Sachi's cell phone, but it had gone immediately to voicemail.

Sachi ... Poonam ... Raveena wondered what they thought.

Even though Siddharth had reciprocated her romantic advances, she felt horribly guilty. It was her idea to stop at the Bandstand. Why couldn't she have seduced him at the Taj Hotel? In one of those gorgeous private rooms?

Randy's secretary, Millie, called to say the shoot was canceled, as Siddharth was unavailable.

At least Millie was sympathetic. "I'm so sorry, ma'am; the police have harassed many couples at the Bandstand. Smooching should not be considered indecent behavior."

"Thank you, Millie," Raveena said.

She spent the rest of the day hanging around the bungalow. In the afternoon, another newspaper was delivered, the *Mid-day*. Raveena had never checked it out before, but she did now, standing on the porch.

On the front page:

BANI SEN DEFENDS SIDDHARTH!

Raveena Rai is nothing but a skanky Yank! Her behavior may be fine in America, but our morals are higher in India. Siddharth was merely giving Raveena a ride home when she began molesting him. The only thing he is guilty of is being a gentleman. And I should know! Siddharth and I are engaged.

Raveena nearly fainted.

Chapter 39

Raveena put her hair in a ponytail and slipped on sunglasses, though she doubted anyone would recognize her. It was just her name that was spread out over the gossip pages.

At the Internet Café she sent out numerous emails to Maza, Jai, Rahul and her parents, begging for guidance, reassurance, comfort, anything.

She would have called, but it was almost three in the morning back in the States, and she couldn't get ahold of Rahul in Brussels.

Depressed, she trudged back to Uncle Heeru's. Not even a cold bottle of Thums Up could rouse her spirits.

Desperate and still depressed, she finally sought out Uncle Heeru. She needed someone, anyone, to talk to.

Heeru was upstairs feeding the birds. She took a seat on the edge of the bed. "Uncle Heeru, there's something I have to tell you."

He pushed his glasses up the bridge of his nose and waited.

Off topic: As soon as she got home, Raveena was sending her uncle a new pair of eyeglasses from Lens-Crafter.

Raveena took a deep breath. "You're going to read some pretty bad things about me in the paper. See, I made a mistake. I, ah, found myself liking Siddharth—the actor—and I thought he liked me too. But it turns out he's engaged. And yesterday we were arrested—it was a trumped-up charge—but some reporter took a photo of us exiting the police station."

Uncle Heeru sat down in a chair across from her, the bag of birdseed in his lap. A pigeon flew in and perched on his head. "I told you this is a bad country. First I am arrested as a spy for Pakistan, and now my niece is arrested. But then you should not have gotten involved with this actor. They are the worst, raping young girls in the studios . . . but then, you will not find success with any man."

"Why?"

Uncle Heeru shifted and the bag of birdseed fell off his lap and spilled across the floor.

Suddenly the floor was covered in pecking pigeons.

Raveena tucked her feet under her. "Why, Uncle Heeru?"

"What?" He stared at her puzzled. "Oh yes," he nodded. "You see there is a curse on our family."

A curse? Was he for real?

Oh, right, this was Uncle Heeru.

"Thirty years ago, my mother owned a beautiful flat on Marine Drive. However, before she could rent it out, squatters took possession of it. Nothing could get rid of them. Not a court ordinance, not the duffers who called themselves police, nothing. Finally, she hired *goondas* to take care of the problem."

"Criminals?" Raveena asked.

"Yes, yes, hired guns," Uncle Heeru said nonchalantly.

If Raveena weren't so depressed she would have laughed at her uncle's use of the term "hired guns."

"The *goondas* banged into the flat and scared the squatters into leaving. Unfortunately, they caused more damage to the property than the squatters. The head of the squatting family was an old woman. She had the face of a *churail*, a witch. She placed a curse on my family. None of my mother's granddaughters would ever marry. They would stay spinsters forever."

Raveena found the curse sexist.

"So, did the witch's words pan out?"

Heeru nodded. "My brothers and sisters have a total of ten girls. All are of marriageable age. All have circled the globe looking for mates. All are still searching. Of course, my nieces are also spoiled, bad-tempered, unattractive girls."

"But Uncle Heeru, I'm not really your niece," Raveena pointed out. "I mean, we're very distantly related."

"You are unlucky in love, no?"

"Yeah."

He held out his hands, palms facing upwards, as if to say, "see?"

Raveena rose. "Thanks for the talk."

Uncle Heeru stood as well, nearly stepping on a pigeon. Said pigeon began angrily pecking on his bare toe.

"When you first arrived, Lavinia, I knew . . . ."

"Knew what?"

"That you should never have come. Bombay is a bad place. The film industry is no place for a young woman."

Biting down on her lip, sidestepping pigeons, Raveena quietly left the room.

Chapter 40

Shooting resumed a week later.

Raveena was surprised at not having received a single email from any friends or family members.

Veer and Lollipop showed their support with kind words and, in Lollipop's case, multiple exuberant hugs. Audrey, the makeup artist, kept bringing Raveena bottles of Thums Up while she sat in the makeup chair.

Randy was the same as ever.

She'd been a bit nervous at facing Daddy, but he was in London attending the wedding of a relative.

And Siddharth . . .

Siddharth completely ignored her.

She knocked on his trailer to no avail. He avoided her on the set. And even during their scenes together, he remained as aloof in character as he was out of it.

Randy didn't even notice.

To make matters worse, Bani Sen was a regular visitor to the set.

When she wasn't with Siddharth, she was keeping an eagle eye on him.

It was especially humiliating for Raveena to watch as studio personnel asked Bani for autographs, and Randy practically tripped over himself trying to make her comfortable.

Bani didn't say anything to Raveena. Her triumphant look was statement enough.

Once, while Raveena was practicing her lines, she overheard Bani remarking to Siddharth, "Her Hindi is terrible . . . what an accent. Did you hear the way she said, Alladin? It's Allah-din, not A-lad-in."

Yes, Randy had added a magic carpet ride to the script, with Alladin making a guest appearance at Shah Jahan's palace.

Even though Siddharth didn't respond to Bani's comment, it still stung.

Raveena would have loved to have made fun of Bani's English, but it was perfect.

Damn colonialism!

At the end of the week, Veer and Randy got into a big argument. The tall Sikh stood his ground, insisting there were continuity problems and they needed to re-shoot several scenes. Randy refused, saying they would go over budget. When Veer demanded Randy call up Daddy in London, Randy refused.

Veer quit.

Raveena ran outside where Veer was leaning against the wall and having a cigarette.

"You can't quit," she cried out. "You're the only one who can save this film."

"I can't work with the man. The relationship between the director and cinematographer needs to be one of communication and shared vision. That chubby bastard doesn't know what the hell he's doing."

"Veer," Raveena protested.

"I'm sorry," he sighed. "My wife will be happy, though. I've been wanting to direct my own film, and she's encouraging me to do so. Looks like I'll have my chance now. I'm in talks with a producer down South."

Raveena sighed and leaned on the wall next to him. "Well, I'm glad I had the chance to work with you. I know you'll make a wonderful director."

"And you, Raveena," Veer turned and faced her, his expression serious, "are a good actress. Don't let anyone tell you otherwise. You're leagues above Bani Sen."

"Thank you, Veer."

As he walked away, Raveena called out the traditional Sikh farewell, "*Sat-sri-akal.*"

Veer turned back and folded his hands. "*Sat-sri-akal.*"

Chapter 41

Raveena's mother called that night.

"Mom! Why didn't you email me back?" Raveena demanded.

"What email?" Leela asked. "I didn't receive one."

Damn Hotmail!

This had happened to Raveena before.

"Are you invited to the wedding?" her mother asked.

"What?"

"I was reading on the *Filmfare* website that Siddharth and Bani Sen are engaged." She sighed. "Such a beautiful couple. Surely, as his costar, you'll be invited to the wedding. All the stars will be there: Shah Rukh, Hrithik, Sanjay Dutt, Aishwariya, Rani Mukherjee . . ."

Raveena felt as though she were going to gag. If only her mother knew the real Bani Sen. Then again, maybe Bani and Siddharth deserved each other.

"Mom, I have to go. Are you and Dad okay?"

"Your father! He made such a mess in the kitchen this morning. And he broke the DVD player! Imagine that! The man is an engineer, and he doesn't even know how to use the DVD?"

All too soon, her mother had to hang up and run errands, and Raveena was left standing in the hall alone.

She tried to give herself another pep talk.

"You didn't come here to hook up with guys. You came to further your career," she said aloud.

Her pep talk sucked.

All she could think about was Siddharth. The man was an ass.

But he still deserved better than Bani.

Raveena hesitated for a moment, then grabbed the phone and punched in all the digits required to call America.

She would pay Uncle Heeru back.

The phone rang and rang. "Pick up, Maza," Raveena whispered.

"Hello?"

"Maza!"

Finally! Maza would give Raveena the pep talk she needed. After all, wasn't Maza off men? Her friend would put things in perspective, as usual.

"Chica! Oh my god, I just walked in the door. Ian and I were going to call you!"

"Ian?"

Maza giggled.

Raveena knew something was very wrong.

Maza never giggled.

"Ian . . ." Maza giggled again. "Ian is my husband."

This time Raveena was the one who dropped the phone.

Moments later she was able to choke out the words. "What? Husband? What are you talking about?"

"I was doing a reading in Seal Beach when this tall blond guy—you know I don't like blonds—comes up to me. Turns out he's a fan . . . well, we went for coffee, coffee turned into drinks, drinks turned into dinner, and forty-eight hours later, chica, we were in Vegas."

"Wow . . . Maza!"

"Ian teaches anthropology at UCLA. I can't wait for you to meet him. We're on our way to my parents' in Santa Barbara. But we won't have the wedding reception until you get back. I need my girl with me. I never in my life thought this would happen. You know me and marriage. And Ian can't wait to meet you."

Raveena felt wretched. She wanted to be happy for her best friend. Instead, she felt jealous. She felt alone.

"So how's Siddharth?" Maza asked.

"Fine," Raveena said. "Look, I have to go. Uncle Heeru needs to use the phone."

"Okay, chica, I'll call you from Santa Barbara."

It's hard, Raveena thought, when the fact that you're a loser seems to be staring you in the face.

"What the bloody hell is your problem?" Sachi demanded, glaring at her brother. "Are you really marrying that bitch, Bani?"

Siddharth groaned and rubbed his face.

Siddharth, Poonam and his manager, Javed Khan, were at the flat. He hadn't realized Sachi was home.

"Now, now, sweetheart," Javed said to Sachi.

Sachi spun on him. "Don't call me sweetheart. Was this all your idea? It's the stupidest idea I've ever heard."

"Now, darling," Poonam lectured. "Javed knows what's

best for Siddharth. Everyone has forgotten about the police incident, no?"

"But what about Raveena?" Sachi insisted. "No one's told her about this publicity plan. If she and Sid really were engaged in lewd behavior—"

Siddharth glared at her. "Sachi."

"Oh, shut up," she answered. "Obviously you two were locking lips or something. That means you like her and she likes you. Then she has to read in the paper that you're engaged? How do you think that makes her feel?"

"Darling, she has a point," Poonam said to Siddharth. "What about poor Raveena? We must tell her the truth."

"Not yet," Javed instructed. "I'm sure Raveena is a nice girl, but how do we know she won't go to the press? Next thing you know the gossip-mongers will be all over Sid. He's up for a CineStar Award in two days. I don't want anything to hurt his chances."

"Oh, please," Sachi scoffed. "If he's rigged to win, he'll win."

"Ah," Javed wagged his finger, "but the people who've done the rigging may change their mind. I want my boy to get this award."

"Oh dear, what a fuddle," Poonam sighed, lighting up a cigarette. "Darling, do you care for Raveena? You have my blessings if you do."

Siddharth sat back against the sofa cushions. "I do, Ma. I want to take things slow, but yes, I do like her."

"Lovely, darling, I'll start planning the wedding. What's her mother's number in America?"

"Ma!" Siddharth warned.

He turned to his manager. "I'm telling her, Javed. I have to. I've made a mess of everything. I've behaved like a jackass."

"Yes, you have," Sachi agreed.

Javed placed his hand on Siddharth's shoulder. "Please, I only ask that you wait until after the CineStar Awards."

"Fine, but I'm leaving as soon as I get the statue."

"Deal."

"Bani called earlier," Sachi said. "Sid, I think she feels she really is your fiancée. She was saying something about going ring shopping."

Javed looked puzzled. "But she was there when I came up with the publicity idea. She knows the engagement isn't real."

"That girl is unbalanced," Poonam said. "It runs in the family."

"You want me to go with you when you talk to Bani?" Sachi offered. "I can handle her."

Siddharth was tempted. His little sister was a lot tougher than he was. But he had built a career on soundly thrashing the bad guys. "Thanks Sachi." He smiled. "But it's my problem."

"Good, now that mess is settled," Poonam said and picked up a pad and pen. "Darlings, let's start thinking up baby names. I like Tasneem for a girl . . ."

Chapter 42

Raveena got a call that morning from Millie D'Souza.

Randy wanted to see her at his office.

By eleven she was there and Millie was ushering her inside. The secretary wore a sad look. Raveena was going to ask Millie if she was okay, but she didn't get a chance.

This time Randy didn't keep her waiting and buzzed her in immediately.

Before Raveena left the waiting room, Millie put a hand on her arm. "Ma'am, I think you're a fine actress."

Raveena shot her a puzzled smile. "Thank you."

Randy indicated Raveena should have a seat and she did.

From his desk he removed an envelope with the Swiss Airlines logo on the front.

"Planning a trip?" Raveena asked.

"To Zurich," Randy said. "I'm going for a holiday."

"When?"

"I'm leaving right after the CineStar Awards."

"But what about the film? It's not finished."

"It's merely a four-day trip," he said and added in a suggestive voice, "and three long nights."

Raveena ignored the suggestion. "Well, I hope you have fun."

Randy rubbed his chin and pushed the tickets towards her. "I have two first-class tickets here. I'd like you to join me."

Oh, so *now* he was offering up first class!

"I don't think so, Randy. We should keep this professional."

"But this *is* professional," he said. "It has everything to do with the movie and your role in it."

"Excuse me?"

"You want to act in my film. And I want to enjoy Zurich with you."

Raveena felt coldness seep into her. "Are you saying you want me to sleep with you? And if I don't, I'm out of the picture?"

The casting couch was finally waiting for her to take a seat.

"I'm tired of waiting for you to come to your senses, Raveena. Why do you think you were chosen for my film? You're nobody in Hollywood *and* Bollywood. The only reason you're here is because I fancy you.

The coldness inside Raveena turned into white hot fury.

She stood up. If there had been a glass of water on his desk, she would have flung the contents in his face. As it were, there was a jar of pens. She picked it up and threw it at him. One of the pens hit Randy on the forehead. "Hey!" he cried.

Raveena gripped the edge of the desk and leaned forward. With his hand pressed against his face, Randy tried to see down her shirt.

195

Raveena threw the stapler at him.

"Listen, asshole. If the choice was between you and that leper with boils who stands on the corner of Turner Road, I still wouldn't sleep with you." She leaned closer. "You're nasty, conniving, pathetic, and I hate you. I hate Bollywood. Fuck all of you!"

"You're fired!" Randy shouted. "I'm hiring Bani Sen. She came to me yesterday and offered to star in my film. She was always my first choice. Bani is a star. You can't even act!"

Raveena looked around, but there was nothing left to throw.

She did, however, slam the door on her way out and didn't reply to Millie's concerned good-bye.

Chapter 43

Newspapers carried reports that it was the hottest day in Bombay that year.

Raveena wandered the streets, the heat adding to her anger and making her head spin, moving aimlessly in no particular direction.

At one point she thought she saw Siddharth walking ahead of her on Linking Road and pushed ahead, trying to see past the waves of people.

The man turned around and Raveena dived behind a coconut juice vendor.

It wasn't Siddharth.

Oh, the humiliation.

Raveena felt a sharp sting and rubbed a weird swollen bump on her neck.

The juice vendor was watching her. Angrily, she stood and continued down the street. Passing by a stack of newspapers, she saw Bani Sen's face. The caption read:

Bani's saying bye-bye to Bollywood?

Raveena grabbed the paper and began scanning.

India's sweetheart Bani Sen has been hand-picked to star in Goldie Hawn's next film. Laughing, the scintillating Sen promises she won't forgo Bollywood for Hollywood. "Bombay is my home," she said happily.

Furious, Raveena threw the paper to the ground. If someone like Bani could drop ass-backwards into a role opposite Goldie Hawn while Raveena couldn't even stay on the cast of *Taj Mahal 3000: Unleashed,* then life was seriously screwed up.

It was like Bombay was rejecting her. Rejecting her like a bad donor organ.

While Bani was living the good life, Raveena was running around trying to keep her hands bacteria-free.

Randy's words echoed in her head.

You can't even act!

She'd show him. She'd show all of them.

She'd tried. God, had she tried. And what did she have to show for it?

She'd finished *Hurray for Bollywood.*

And then she walked past a shop where the television was blaring.

Stopping, she stared at the screen. A reporter stood in front of the Andheri Sports Complex.

The CineStar Awards would be held there tonight. Bollywood's glitterati would be in attendance—that meant Siddharth, Bani and Randy Kapoor.

Siddharth was up for a best actor award for *Love in Kashmir.*

The CineStar Awards . . .

Raveena hadn't received an invitation to the show, but a plan began to form in her mind.

According to the reporter, Randy Kapoor would be presenting the Award for best actress.

The reporter also mentioned the stunning lapses in security at the last Awards show.

The universe was giving her a sign.

She looked up at the sky, and an angry smile formed on her lips.

Look out, Bollywood.

Raveena Rai is about to go Quentin Tarantino on your ass!

Chapter 44

Raveena wasn't a wimp.

Neither was she a Sidney Sheldon heroine who could gutsy her way into an editor's office, demand a job, and deliver a top-notch story by somehow staking out the visiting diplomat no one else could get to, all thanks to her brains and ravishing beauty.

But she did manage to sneak into the Andheri Sports Complex without raising any alarms.

Then again, so did about a hundred other uninvited fans and curious onlookers.

The entertainment reporter staking out the aisle got on Raveena's nerves with her incessant chatting. "Ladies and gentleman, expect a wild and wacky night, filled with temperamental and whimsical stars—"

Whimsical? Raveena wondered.

"Stunning gimmicks, special effects and shenanigans galore," the reporter trilled. "The CineStar Awards just infects one with enthusiasm and endearment for what this show means. To honor the best talents and provide encouragement and incentive to all the members of India's Motion Picture Academy."

Raveena wanted to gag.

"So stay tuned for electric excitement, tangible tension, magical moments, poised perfection and scintillating stars."

Raveena nearly wrestled the microphone away from her.

"For the first time in CineStar history, the Awards show will be beamed live to countries all over the world."

On stage, the crew was checking on the sparkling waterfall that stood nearly two stories in height. Technicians in charge of the fireworks display wore black Polo shirts with "Ramani Fireworks" printed on the back.

Raveena suddenly had an idea.

She followed one of the technicians backstage. Once she was sure they were alone, she executed her cunning plan.

She handed the skinny man fifty American dollars. "Can I have your shirt?"

He took the money. "Are you serious?"

"Yes."

He handed her back a ten. "I'll take forty. This shirt itches."

Raveena pocketed the money, and the man peeled off his shirt.

"Here." Raveena peeled off her white Tee, paying no attention to the way the man was ogling her bra-covered breasts.

They walked off in each other's shirts.

Looking like one of the fireworks crew, Raveena moved towards the stage and found a hiding place in a dark corner.

There, she burrowed and waited for her moment.

When Randy Kapoor would take the stage.

Chapter 45

Damn it to hell!

How long was the Awards show anyway?

Three hours into it, her ears ringing with Bollywood hits, Raveena tried to ignore the stiffness in her legs.

Musical performance after musical performance went on with stars lip-synching and dancing to their most popular songs.

Siddharth won for best actor.

Raveena felt a pull in her heart when he walked up on stage. He looked less than enthusiastic and merely thanked the crew and his fans for the Award. He then practically ran off stage.

She longed to go after him.

Was she? Could she be? Bat shit crazy?

Raveena was well-acquainted with bat shit, as the baby fruit bat had left behind a little present in her hair.

And then the host asked Randy Kapoor to please come on stage.

She clenched her teeth as Randy swaggered on stage in

typical asshole fashion. He was chewing gum, which Raveena found utterly tasteless.

The nominees for best actress were read out.

"And now," said the host, a good-looking metrosexual man with a British accent and handsome face. Raveena recognized him as an up-and-comer from Page Three. "Will Mr. Randy Kapoor please read out the winner for best actress?"

Chomping gum, Randy made a big show of opening the envelope.

"Rani Mukherjee!" he crowed.

Raveena liked Rani. The woman was exceptionally talented and spoke with an attractive smoky voice.

Rani graciously accepted her award and exited the stage.

Randy was about to step off too when Raveena lunged and grabbed him.

She pulled out a knife.

Granted, it was a small, dull butter knife from Uncle Heeru's kitchen, but no one could tell from that distance. And Randy was such a coward he wouldn't care.

Raveena turned to the host. "Leave," she ordered.

The young man turned and ran off.

With the butter knife to his throat, Raveena dragged Randy to the podium.

The lights were intense and bright, but she could make out some of the audience. No one seemed to care about what was happening.

"It's an ad break," the host called out from off stage.

So Raveena waited until the break was over and the music started up again.

"Help me!" Randy screamed into the microphone.

There were startled gasps from the audience as people turned their attention back to the show.

Raveena decided to hurry and speak before security rushed the stage.

She pushed Randy down and stepped on his stomach. "If you move, I'll shoot you," she whispered. Obviously it would prove rather difficult to shoot the man with a butter knife, but Randy whimpered like a baby.

"Bollywood," she said into the microphone, "is a disgrace. I know that many of you don't care for the term Bollywood. You feel it demeans the industry. Well, you know what really demeans your industry? The way you rip off Hollywood films!"

The audience was silent.

Security hadn't arrived so Raveena decided to elaborate.

"You guys love to hold yourselves up as virtuous and moral, but I've seen the seamy side of Bollywood. Your heroes and heroines go to the temple, respect their elders and never kiss on screen . . . but what about all the breast shaking and hip thrusting in the songs? You're all hypocrites! And what about the Mafia? How many films do they really finance?"

Raveena quickly decided to lay off the Mafia because she didn't want to get murdered.

"Where's the originality in your industry? One romantic comedy becomes a hit, and suddenly that's all you guys make. One underworld drama becomes a blockbuster, and all the other directors follow suit. So what if you have a billion fans around the world. I'm embarrassed by Bollywood films. I don't want to show them to my friends.

"Look at the way you portray Indians who live abroad.

The girls are westernized and have no morals, while the girls brought up in India are virtuous ladies. That is such bullshit! And you know who the worst offender is? Randy Kapoor. Every single one of his films is a Hollywood rip-off. Frame by frame! I came to Bollywood, and I took a chance. And you know what? Bollywood let me down. How can you people even call yourselves moviemakers?"

From the corner of her eye, Raveena saw security rushing towards her.

"Bollywood sucks!" she screamed and took off.

Apparently, the security guards were out of shape, because minutes later she was running out the back exit of the sports complex.

The enormity of what she had done shook her. She was crying and hyperventilating at the same time. She didn't know where to go.

She plunged down a darkened street.

In the distance, she heard sirens.

Too late, she realized she was heading into the slums.

But there was no turning back.

She ran past crying babies, lethargic mothers, barking dogs and bored men. Stumbling in the darkness, she made her way through the streets, the only light coming from the distance and the small cooking fires burning around her.

Raveena searched for an empty space.

And finally at the end of a row of slum dwellings, she found one.

Chapter 46

Hours later, Raveena was still huddled on the dirt floor of the Bombay slum.

She moved from crouching to a curled-up fetal position. The heavy night air caused trickles of sweat and grime to run down her face.

The sound of voices erupted from outside.

Loud male voices.

The police had found her.

Desperately, she looked around for a place to hide. The only furniture in the room was a shabby straw mat.

She began wriggling her way under the covering just as the door burst open.

Uniformed men with flashlights filled the room and yanked off her hiding place.

She placed a weak hand in front of her eyes to shield them from the glare of the lights.

This was the end.

Raveena didn't know whether to faint or throw up.

"Raveena!"

She heard his voice.

It couldn't be.

She removed her hand and blinked into the light. A tall man stood in front of her, his broad shoulders filling the small space.

"Siddharth?" she whispered.

And for the second time, Raveena burst into tears in front of him.

Chapter 47

Raveena awoke in a cool air-conditioned room in a bed with silken sheets.

The events of the night before washed over her, and she buried her face in the pillow, overcome with embarrassment.

Siddharth had brought her to his home.

Poonam had taken charge, giving Raveena a nightie to change into, fixing her a glass of brandy and hot tea and then sitting with her until she fell asleep.

The bedroom door opened and Siddharth entered.

"Hi," he said shyly.

Raveena sat up and tucked a lock of her hair behind her ear. "Hi . . . I feel like an idiot."

"Don't," Siddharth said. "The papers didn't even cover it."

"What?"

"Well around the same time you took Randy hostage on stage—"

Raveena winced.

"Sorry," Siddharth said. "Well around that time, a major fight broke out between Tiger Patel and Shekhar Suri."

"The actors?"

"They're big-time rivals, and of course Tiger and Shekhar were both drunk as hell. All the reporters were there covering it. So was half the audience. The other half first thought you and Randy were enacting a skit. Then security rushed the stage, you ran off, security rushed back to where Tiger was braining Shekhar, and, well, that was the talk of the night."

"Thank god," Raveena said relieved.

"Your mother called."

"Oh no."

"She called your uncle's place after seeing the show. Apparently she woke up around five a.m. to watch it."

Raveena rolled her eyes.

"When I called your uncle to tell him where you were— by the way, did you know that he thought you were sleeping in your bed?"

"Doesn't surprise me."

"Well, your uncle gave me your mother's number, and I called her."

Raveena watched as Siddharth's golden cheeks turned a rosy red. "What?" she asked.

"Well," he said, "she, ah, got rather excited when she heard my voice."

Raveena took a deep breath. "Listen, Siddharth, I'm so sorry about the police thing. It was my fault for making you stop at the Bandstand. I hope . . ." she had to choke this out, "I hope what happened between us didn't affect your relationship with Bani. Tell her it was pre-wedding jitters or something."

Siddharth frowned. "Bani? Bloody hell, I forgot about

Javed's crazy plan. Listen Raveena, Bani and I were never really engaged. My manager was afraid the police incident would interfere with my chances for the stupid award, so he concocted a story that would get more press than anything. I was going to tell you after the show . . ."

He paused.

"I was stupid for not telling you sooner. It's just, I was so embarrassed about the police thing. I should have handled it better. And then there was the story with Bani and . . . I'm sorry."

Raveena hadn't paid attention to anything he had said beyond, "Bani and I aren't engaged."

Instead, she smiled and nodded. "So you and Bani aren't together," she repeated.

"We never were."

"I was never with Randy."

"I know, Raveena."

Before she could do a jig, Raveena remembered something. "Is Randy going to press charges? I didn't really hurt him. It was just . . . he fired me, you know. After I told him I wouldn't sleep with him."

Siddharth curled his lip. "Bani threw a fit when I reminded her the engagement was just a publicity ploy. I'm afraid she was partly responsible for encouraging Randy to finally go ahead and proposition you."

"And pressing charges?" Raveena asked. "Randy will, won't he?"

Looked like she'd be ending up in front of the Bombay High Court after all.

"I placed a call to Daddy," Siddharth said. "He's flying in tonight. We're going to straighten this mess out."

Slowly, he placed a tentative hand next to hers.

Raveena laid her hand over his.

She really wanted to pull Siddharth down beside her on the bed but decided there would be time for that later.

Chapter 48

Daddy indeed straightened everything out.

He threatened to cut Randy off financially if he even breathed the word "sue." Daddy then pulled funding from *Taj Mahal 3000: Unleashed* and forced his son to look into film schools if he wanted to keep on directing.

Over the next couple of weeks, Daddy rehired the screenwriter who'd come up with the original idea—the one about the Indo-American girl who goes to India to search for her father.

But best of all, Daddy hired a wonderful director, Dharamveer "Veer" Sandhu to direct it.

Veer asked Raveena and Siddharth to play the leads.

Siddharth came on as associate producer and convinced Raveena to stay and give Bollywood another shot.

Raveena really didn't need much convincing.

Daddy called Griffin in LA and a new contract was drafted.

This time Raveena would be making a significantly higher amount of money.

Not enough to live like a demigoddess, but pretty damn good.

Poonam wanted Raveena to move out of Heeru's and stay with them, but she and Siddharth were taking it slow. Sure, there was still a lot of tongue twisting and lip locking between the two of them, but no one was drawing up baby names . . .

Yet.

So Raveena moved to the Regent Hotel overlooking the water on Bandra's Bandstand. Uncle Heeru had offered his bungalow, but Raveena could not resist the lure of air-conditioning.

Besides, this way she could have Siddharth up for a nightcap.

She did, for some odd reason, find herself missing Uncle Heeru at times, and on those occasions, she'd hop into a rickshaw and motor over to his place. There they'd feed the pigeons together and Uncle Heeru would tell her more stories.

Like the time the stone-pelting swami showed up at his bungalow door and demanded that Heeru buy him a microwave.

"But the man lives in a cave," Raveena pointed out. "Where would he plug it in?"

In May, Maza, Ian and Jai flew to Bombay to visit. When Jai met Siddharth, he fainted.

Raveena liked Ian. Around him, Maza did what no one had ever been able to convince her to do.

She lightened up.

In September, Veer announced "It's a wrap."

The film was titled *Cute Curry*.

Early buzz predicted the movie would be the next *Monsoon Wedding*.

Raveena and Siddharth flew to LA to meet her parents and attend Maza and Ian's reception bash in Santa Barbara.

When Raveena's mother met Siddharth she didn't faint, but she did show him off at her kitty party.

Auntie Kiran took one look at Siddharth and announced that maybe India wasn't such a dirty stinking place after all.

And neither was Bollywood.

Want More?

Turn the page to enter
Avon's Little Black Book—

the dish, the scoop and the
cherry on top from
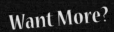
SONIA SINGH

BOLLYWOOD 101

As much as I lampoon and disparage Bollywood movies, I love them with all the secret passion of a forty-year-old man hoarding Hello Kitty. The music, the costumes, the heroes and heroines of Bollywood films have as much a place in my journey from childhood to adulthood as Judy Blume books, the Chronicles of Narnia and the entire series of Sweet Valley High.

Now, considering the Indian film industry produces upwards of a thousand movies a year, and taking into account how I've been watching said movies for about thirty years, that's about thirty thousand movies.

I'm wondering if I have time to review all of them.

Hmm, according to my editor . . . I most certainly do not.

Okay, so instead I'm going to name my top ten favorite Bollywood flicks of all time. It's no coincidence that these same films also contain my favorite Bollywood soundtracks of all time. Because make no mistake about it: without Bollywood music there is no Bollywood cinema.

After you go through my top ten list you may find yourself consumed with a fervent desire to see a Bollywood film, but where can you find one? Well, either head to your nearest Indian store or shop online (Netflix carries Bollywood DVDs), or to the nearest movie theater playing a Bollywood film. If you choose the latter, do not, I repeat, DO NOT, decide to make a first date out of it. The average Bollywood film is three hours long. What if halfway through you find yourself detesting the person? What if halfway through you realize that you'd rather consume an entire tub of lard than spend one more minute with this person?

See what I mean?

Yes, I realize you could always walk out of the theater or ask the date to please leave . . .

But that would be impolite.

Now, in no particular order, let's get on with the list!

1. **Dilwale Dulhania Le Jayenge** (1995) "Those with heart shall take the bride." I saw this movie four times. It became one of the biggest Indian hits of all time and is my favorite Bollywood film. It stars the delectable Shah Rukh Khan, who also happens to be my favorite Bollywood star. The story is about two Indian kids, Raj and Simran, who live in London with their families. The two meet while on a Eurail trip through Europe with their respective friends and experience the entire gamut of emotions. First they hate each other, then they reluctantly respect each other, then they become friends with each other, and by the end of the trip they fall in love. Unfortunately, Simran's family has arranged her marriage to a boy in India, and when her father discovers she's fallen in love with another, he whisks her off to the golden fields of Punjab. It is now up to Raj to follow her to India, win over Simran's family and claim the girl of his dreams.

2. **Sholay** (1975) "Flames." If you had to ask the average Indian what his or her favorite Bollywood movie is, you'd probably hear about *Sholay*. *Sholay* is based on Kurosawa's magnificent *Seven Samurai*. I just, um, kinda wish the Indian filmmakers had gotten permission from Kurosawa. Despite that, this is probably one of the best remakes in Bollywood history. The story revolves around two small-time crooks who are picked by the former police officer who sent them to jail to defend his village against the sinister bandit Gabbar Singh (no relation to yours truly). This is the only Bollywood film where I

cried at the end. The movie also stars Amitabh Bachan, a living legend in India and voted "star of the millennium" by a BBC poll, beating out Lawrence Olivier!

3. **Kuch Kuch Hota Hai** (1998) "Something happens . . ." Part of me did not want to put this movie in with the others because while in Bombay I ran into the director at a trendy restaurant. He bumped me, spilled my drink and walked off without apologizing . . . but *I'll* be the bigger person. In 1998 two films became the highest grossing box office hits in Indian history. One was *Titanic*. The other was *KKHH*. This film also stars my adorable Shah Rukh Khan. I saw this movie twice because the first time the Indian lady sitting behind me in the theater had to translate the entire film to her non-Indian friend. The ENTIRE 180-minute film! I shushed her until my mouth was raw, but to no avail. The story revolves around a little girl who opens a series of letters from her dead mother on her eighth birthday. The letters tell the story of Anjali, Rahul and Tina, three happy-go-lucky college students. Too late, Anjali realizes she's in love with her best friend, Rahul, just as he realizes he's in love with the beautiful new girl, Tina. The little girl reading the letters is Tina and Rahul's daughter. And in the letters Tina tells her daughter to find Anjali and bring her and Rahul back together. The whole audience was bawling throughout the movie. All except for the annoying woman who kept on translating.

4. **Bombay** (1995) This movie isn't your typical love story. Well, it has a love story, but its main message is political. It was made by one of the most talented directors in India, Mani Ratnam. The music was composed by the brilliant A.R. Rahman. Rahman has sold more CDs than Madonna and Britney Spears combined! He also composed the music for the Andrew Lloyd Webber musical *Bombay Dreams*. The movie *Bombay* stars the ethereally beautiful Manisha, who also happens to be a member of the Nepalese ruling family. Based on true events, Bombay

begins as a poignant love story between a Hindu man and a Muslim woman   a taboo in the small village they hail from. Against family wishes, they marry and move to Bombay. A few years later the Bombay riots break out, pitting Hindu against Muslim. The director's message is simple: You're not Hindu. You're not Muslim. You're all Indians. I think the director deserves snaps for touching a subject the rest of the industry was too afraid to touch.

5. **Lagaan** (2001) "Land tax." Ooh, I was so thrilled when this Bollywood movie was nominated for best foreign film at the Academy Awards! When the handsome star and producer of the film, Aamir Khan, walked the red carpet, I was so proud! Once again the music was composed by the brilliant A.R. Rahman! *Lagaan* takes place in the time of the British Raj. The monsoon has failed to come, and the farmers of a small village hope they'll be excused from paying the crippling land tax the British rulers have imposed. Instead, the British officer in charge surprisingly challenges them to a game of cricket, a game alien and unknown to them. If they win, they get their wish; if they lose, however, the increased tax burden will destroy their lives. The people are terrified, but one man thinks the challenge is worth staking their entire future on. And he convinces the villagers to give it their best shot.

6. **Karz** (1980) "Karmic debt." This is another great film that veers from the typical love story formula. Ravi is a very wealthy, but not very observant, young man who's just married Kamini and takes her on a tour of his tea estate in the beautiful hill station of Ooty on their second day of marriage. As soon as Ravi gets out of the car to stretch his legs, Kamini jumps behind the wheel and runs him over—again and again—until the poor guy's white cashmere sweater is stained with blood. Kamini then gleefully kicks out Ravi's old widowed mother and his unmarried sister from the family mansion. Twenty years

later, Monty, a singing sensation, comes to Ooty in pursuit of a cute girl he met at a party. There he begins to have visions of another life and slowly comes to realize he is the reincarnation of Ravi. He decides it's time to settle things with Kamini and restore his mother (still alive) and sister (aged maid servant) to their family home. There is a scene where Monty enters the hut where "his" old mother is living and she recognizes Ravi in him and begins crying. I think this was taken from a movie called *The Reincarnation of Peter Proud*. Needless to say, I saw that movie when I was a kid, and Peter shouldn't be too proud of it. *Karz* is a much better film.

7. **Lawaaris** (1981) "Orphan." This movie also stars Amitabh Bachan—the actor of the millennium—and it is one of his biggest hits. Amitabh plays a boy whose unwed mother dies, and he is sent to be raised by a drunken bum. One of my favorite scenes is where the young boy is sitting on a roadside crying because he's alone and hungry, and a stray dog steals a piece of naan from a restaurant and carries it back for the boy. I cried in that scene. Later, the boy meets the daughter of wealthy parents, she gives him food and money, and they become best friends. Unfortunately, fate separates them and the boy is once again alone. I didn't really cry in that scene. Anyway, the boy grows up and discovers he is the illegitimate son of a wealthy industrialist. He also falls in love with a beautiful young woman who turns out to be his childhood friend! The young woman is played by actress Zeenat Aman—in my opinion (and that's what this whole list is) the most stunning Bollywood actress ever. Anyway, how the orphan finds the secret of his parentage and brings about a family reunion forms the rest of the story.

8. **Qurbani** (1980) "Sacrifice." This movie also stars the beautiful Zeenat Aman. Zeenat dared to wear a bikini in the film, and the Indian censors went crazy! *Qurbani* is considered one of the classic Bollywood action films

with its tale of shootouts, brawls, car chases, double-crosses, nasty villains, nastier vamps and a stunning heroine. It also has two heroes who are on the wrong side of the law but on the right side of honor. If you ever wondered what would happen if disco and Bollywood came together, you have to listen to this movie's sound-track. It's groovy with a side of curry! Rajesh is a master thief who spits in the eye of death and danger while calmly puffing on a smoke and keeping his shirt half buttoned to display his hairy chest. He only steals from the bad guys, though, and sticks up for the less fortunate. Amar is a gold smuggler who dispatches hooligans with his fists of fury, all while carrying his little daughter on his back. The scariest villain is Princess Jwala who has creepy green cat eyes and handles a machine gun and a bulldozer with equal aplomb. On a side note, I distinctly remember the scene where Amar stumbles into a room covered in blood, and I screamed "ketchup man." Huh.

9. Mr. India (1987) This movie was directed by Shekhar Kapur, who went on to direct Cate Blanchett in *Elizabeth* and Kate Hudson in *Four Feathers*. *Mr. India* also veered from the Bollywood love story formula by mixing in elements of science fiction. Arun, who plays Mr. India, adopts abandoned children and looks after them in the house that he rents. Seema, the heroine, is an intrepid journalist who rents a room from Arun. One day, Arun's deceased father's friend reveals to Arun that his father had a secret formula that can make any human being become invisible. Arun obtains this formula and uses his invisibility to beat evil gangsters, in particular Mr. Mogambo, at their own game. Mr. Mogambo is a nasty rich tycoon who plans to become the ruler of India and indulge his greed. With his access to the invisibility formula, only Arun has the power to stop him. Arun makes his presence known to other people by calling himself Mr. India and never revealing his real name. Under this pretense, Mr. India bumps into and charms

Seema, who falls in love with him. Little does she
realize that the great and elusive Mr. India is actually
her landlord.

10. **Darr** (1993) "Fear." This film ALSO stars my favorite,
Shah Rukh Khan. This film helped propel Khan to the
top, and he deserved everything he got because no Bollywood actor would touch the role. Why? Bollywood stars
only want to play heroes, not villains. But Shah Rukh
said yes to the part and the rest is history. Today Shah
Rukh Khan is probably the top box office attraction in
Bollywood. In this thriller, he plays a young man, Rahul,
dangerously obsessed with winning the heart of a college
girl, Kiran, who plans to marry another. Love . . .
Passion . . . Obsession. This obsession causes Rahul to
take daring steps to prevent Kiran from marrying naval
officer Sunil, and when she finally does, his fury causes
him to break all limits . . .

Well, there you have it, my top ten Bollywood favorites.
I'm very proud of my list, and not just because it took me a
long time to write. Like many of the heroes and heroines in
the Bollywood films, my relationship with the Indian film
industry is one of hate that grew into love that led to
misunderstandings and separation, but eventually we came
back together and lived happily ever after.

SONIA SINGH

SONIA SINGH lives in Orange County, California, with her cat Kali Mata. When not writing books, she dances in front of the mirror in imitation of a belly-baring Bollywood babe.

AVON TRADE... because every great bag deserves a great book!

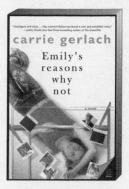
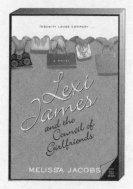